WRITING THAT RISKS

WRITING THAT RISKS

new work from beyond the mainstream

edited by
LIANA HOLMBERG and
DEBORAH STEINBERG

rb

RED BRIDGE PRESS
San Francisco, CA

This anthology contains fiction, poetry, and essays. All events and characters portrayed in these works are fictitious or used fictitiously.

Red Bridge Press
P.O. Box 591104
San Francisco, CA 94159
www.redbridgepress.com

This book is available in print and electronic formats. It can be ordered from redbridgepress.com, online book retailers, and most bookstores, and it can be downloaded to most e-reading devices.

Library of Congress Control Number 2013910591
ISBN 978-0-9894251-0-0

Book cover and interior design by Tina Henderson
Cover photo © Viktor Gladkov | Dreamstime.com
Copyediting by Lavonne Leong

For Alex.

—L. H.

In memory of Lillian Morgan.

—D. S.

Contents

Introduction

We are awash in an ocean of influences—from *The Metamorphosis* to the Matrix—colliding currents that churn up strange connections and unexpected insights. Yet few writers explore these rich confluences, sticking instead to the familiarity of mainstream realism. At Red Bridge Press, we love great writing, no matter the genre, but we wanted to know what would happen if writers were given permission to go farther. Where would they go? What would they see? What would they bring back?

We put out a broad call for "writing that risks," curious to see how it would be interpreted. The response exceeded all our hopes, and we received almost five hundred submissions by brand-new to well-established authors. Their work ranged from surreal to experimental and fabulist to slipstream, with some that fit no category. Many of the authors told us these pieces were the closest to their hearts but the hardest to get mainstream publishers to take a chance on. It turns out that's just what we were looking for. Our first step in winnowing the submissions was to select work that demonstrated solid literary craft and took interesting risks with style and content. From this list, we chose the pieces that most challenged, delighted, and moved us. The result is the anthology before you.

The writing in this book does indeed go farther. It also looks closer, undaunted by the strangeness and inconsistencies that riddle reality. In these stories, you'll meet a boy trying to hold his family together, whose story reveals itself only through erasure; a girl seeking shelter in a near future when the weather's moods can kill; and a woman before the gates of Heaven who won't let God off the hook. Two pieces of memoir will enchant you with a mix of fantasy and reality, all while breathing new life into the form. Among the verse, you'll get inside a poem co-created by iPhone apps, travel to Hong Kong to stand under the "only cubist lamppost in the world," and unimagine the color blue.

These are some of the most unique voices available in print. The twenty-nine authors collected here hail from six countries and fourteen U.S. states, speak many languages, and belong to multiple cultures and communities. Each author takes us on a journey that brings us back to ourselves. Enriched with words full of humor and humanity, we see our lives as they really are: abundant, irreplaceable, and more than a little odd.

Liana Holmberg
San Francisco, CA

DEAR MONDAY

Christina Olson

A found poem composed of lines from e-mails sent 2007–2011.

Dear Monday, we are getting divorced. I hope
this Halloween nobody tells you how big
your boobs are, and I hope you get really loaded
and say the word *fuck* to a bunch of trick or treaters.
In the hallway, I passed some kid complaining
about his roommate not doing the dishes and he said
I was like, I have to do both the wash
AND *the dry? What am I, a fucking single mom?*

I find myself dizzy a lot these days.
It's really weird, like I'm walking around
sort of drunk even though I'm sober.
It's just the feeling of being so tired
and then feeling like there is no forseeable time
when I will not be so tired.
I don't think we'll ever be adults.

So it goes, weird spring, with your sunny weather
and frigid temperatures and people dying
all the time. Oh my god, it just keeps snowing
and snowing and snowing. Most of the time
February makes me want to kill myself.
Twice over. That's all. It's hard,
and I don't like it. But think about June,
with so many fresh tomatoes
we'll bleed tiny white seeds
if we cut ourselves. How can I worry,
when that is all that matters?

I wish there was a training class for me
each time I went through a life adjustment:
This is how to stop crying,
this is how to stop spending all of your money,
this is how to make your favorite drinks more alcoholic.
Or, if you need to laugh at something,
then think about that image in my head
I keep having of being absent and putting
a sandwich on the table and saying,
This is your sub, see you Monday.
If we're ever adults, I'll hate us.

When I went to church on Sunday, I saw a book
entitled *The Living Bible* propped up on the table
in the vestibule. What astonished me
was the subtitle, in neat little print:
paraphrased. You know, I think
a lot of the Bible loses its power
when you start paraphrasing. Jesus
and some dudes hanging out on a beach
just doesn't really do much for me.

I tried to get happy, I really did.
I took the dog to the park and he rolled
in geese shit. Now my brain
feels as though it is pulsing like in cartoons
where brains are huge and usually evil.
Then the squirrels got into the garbage
while it was sitting on the curb and rolled
the container into the street and a truck
drove over it. In conclusion,
I want a new pair of shoes.

DISPLAY WINGS

David Ellis Dickerson

I: Friday's Admiral

Mr. Quincunx jerks his halberd at me. "Collect all our wonders of Egypt in this room. I want the earliest wonders on that end"—a jab at the corner—"and the later wonders here." The halberd slices air, a piece of dying sunlight at its tip. "And I want the Upper Nile on *this* side and the Lower Nile on *that* side." (Jab, jab.) "Tonight is perilous, and I've got lots to do. Don't make me tell you twice."

Behind me, Muenster says, "Tick tick tick tick tick . . . "

Quincunx glares him into silence. The haft drums once against the tile and he's off through the east door, down the hall, epaulets tinkling. We don't bother to ask our questions, viz.:

Why wear a naval cap?

When is the Rabble coming? Will they hurt us or let us go?

Shouldn't we board the windows first?

What was wrong with the old way?

Or the pair of questions that's been nagging me for months now: *What does this museum actually accomplish? What if we deserve to be destroyed and we don't even know it?*

The Q vanishes from view with a sharp, boot-clicking left. We hear echoes of stairs being reverentially pounded. Muenster stabs his dying cheroot against the chess case and snorts. "The whole museum? Jesus Christ. I hope he's telling other docents the same thing."

"I'm worried about the sarcophagi," I say. "And me with my back."

"And now this is the Egypt Room," says Muenster. "Time marches on."

"It's not supposed to," I say. "Not here." I prefer the old name for this room: The Annex of Miscellany. That's been its name for ten generations. It's my favorite spot. Why change now?

"Is he like this with everybody, you think?" says Muenster. "I mean tonight?"

"Maybe he's mad with power. The uniform?"

"Huh. I bet it was when they deputized him. He already had a uniform."

I shrug. "Maybe it's the epaulets." Quincunx has high shoulders and a neck so stunted the epaulets neighbor his ears. I imagine them singing to him, *Your country needs you. Civilization is crying for help. Only you can produce and/or preserve culture.* It must be a tempting melody. "Maybe he's just scared. I hear he used to be a lawyer, but something happened." There's no way to prepare for this life. Most of us tumbled here from someplace more profane.

But Muenster's not listening. He scowls at where the halberd just swung, fidgeting with thick fingers. He looks angry, which means he's uncertain.

"It's simple," I say, and with my finger in the dust above the Lepidoptera I draw a diagram on the glass:

UP   OLD

NEW   LOW

Really it's just an excuse to trail my fingers over the butterflies. I love their names: *Friday's admiral, pale crescent, question mark,* etc. I feel that if I read them in the proper order, I might be able to tell my own fortune. Or that touching their names would give me their properties. Iconology breeds animism. I can feel it building in me every day, and sometimes it's all I can do not to bow down to a totem, using it properly for once.

"Says you," says Muenster. "With just the two of us, how do we move everything? Where do we put the remainder?"

I hadn't thought that far. "Let's divide up, and move small things first. You go around and grab Nile objects from the other rooms. I'll take stuff from . . . "

"Jesus!" Muenster looks at the ceiling. "I think I hear the Rabble."

"That's just boiling. Don't you ever cook?"

His hand chops to quiet me. We stand there. The roof doesn't collapse. "I hope they come," said Muenster. "We're sure as hell ready."

" . . . I'll take non-Egyptian stuff from here and look for places to put it. We'll start small."

"But!" Muenster flails at everything. "That sarcophagus! The stuffed ibises! The butterfly case!"

"We're deputized. There's always a lot of volunteers working the weekends, especially just before a big exhibit opens."

"The whale!" Muenster snaps his fingers.

I nod. "I say we recruit people if we meet any."

A smile spreads across his face, a crack widening in a malt-colored soufflé. Maybe he won't have to carry anything! "High Nile," he says. "Where's a dolly?"

"Closet. The big one."

He clomps to the door, stops, and turns with another seasick grin. "The easiest way to do this, you know, would be to just switch all the labels."

"You lazy prick."

"The Rabble would never know the difference. They'll take anything we say."

I reply with a silent stare. If the Rabble did anything we said, they wouldn't be rioting right now and we wouldn't have all these crazy precautions. Tomorrow we could both be out of a job and back with the groundlings, the very thought of which makes my throat pulse.

"Yeah, well . . . " Muenster says, and vanishes down the hall. His saber is slung low, and long after he leaves I can hear the scabbard's iron tip scraping. I imagine sparks.

I figure I'll start light, carry the fragile stuff while I'm still alert. I seize a tan Chinese funerary urn (Western Jin dynasty; glazed, and sporting pictures of birds) and a Japanese dish (Arita ware from the Saga prefecture; featuring a horse-like dragon dancing under blossoming cherry trees). Ensuring my grip, I freeze and listen for the approaching riot—primitive instincts seem alive tonight—but all I hear is the boil-

ing from the roof. Before I leave I draw another note in the dust above
the butterflies:

M.—

THE IBISES DON'T MOVE.

—N.

II: Pale Crescent

At dusk, the main hall is the most beautiful part of the museum. Espe-
cially at this time of day and this time of year, when you can look out one
of the vaulted west windows and see the last bald tip of the lowering sun,
and then you can look out one of the east windows and see the unprepos-
sessing moon. My favorite thing to do when this happens is to walk to the
far end, facing the entrance, and pretend this is an old Greek colonnade,
just deserted, but with all the different voices of the agora still collid-
ing in echoes. It feels that way this time of year—you can stand facing
the entrance with your back to The Whale Experience, The Map Room,
The Hall of Oddities & Wonders, just staring out into the real workaday
world and watch the dust motes whirl in this conversation of light. At
times like this, you can pretend that all times are like this. That's what
I love about working in the museum: it proves that, under certain con-
trolled conditions, time can be perfect—quiet, nostalgic, unthreatening.

I stood in line waiting to get in when I was so small I had to reach up
to feel the gold ropes. Back then, I couldn't wait to see everything. Now
I frown at how many stand here staring at the doors that hide the first
collection and miss the different beauties outside the museum, stream-
ing in like light. I used to think this place was exciting and important,
with all these frozen artifacts captured in a vital moment, as if they were
holding their breath and readying themselves impatiently for the next
startling gesture. But if you hold your breath long enough you simply
stop breathing. If the guests knew how ignorant and disorganized we
all are, always one original question shy of exposure. How often I stand
here and try to recapture my wonder.

Tonight, though, I cannot stay. The low glints of light outside the windows might be stars, or they might be approaching torches. I tell myself it's best to keep busy, and not to think about what everything means.

III: Question Mark

Now past the Whale Experience, along rows of ploughshares, sharp right at the Mineral Specularium, through a stern wooden door (BY PERMISSION ONLY), down the stairs to the cellar level, teapot and urn and me. This is where we're going to keep the porcelain from now on—Japanese to the east, China in the middle, European and Sundry Others in the west wing. Where not just anyone can come in.

Unless, of course, one sneaked in from below. It's possible. There's another door in this room leading farther down, god knows where. Quincunx always warned me not to go deeper than the first basement. "No one's been down there in decades," he said, clipped and remorseless. "It's probably filled with poisonous snakes."

Tonight I am tempted. I set the teapot and urn on a nearby table and I move aside some crates and open the door. There is no light: the lower levels rely on nonexistent torches in empty sconces. I can only see a few stone stairs that change to wood and circle underneath where I'm standing. Even the air is empty—no dust, no dankness. Perhaps there is a vent.

The museum was built on the site of Ye Olde Collection House, which was swallowed in an earthquake before Mr. Quincunx's predecessor was born. The Collection House was, in turn, built on top of a Castle of Wonders, which sank after some flooding. The Castle itself was selected, rumor has it, because its site was the same as an old Roman tower that was driven like a spike into the ground by a stray meteor. This museum is who knows how many buried stories deep. Who knows what someone else might build on its retired shoulders.

I've never been down there. If the mob comes and destroys us, there will never be another chance. Tonight, then, definitely. It is narrow enough that I can touch both walls with either hand and still make my way one tentative step at a time.

It smells anticlimactic, as if the air holds no surprises and what am I bothering for? I walk downstairs and, after the first turn of the stair, with the dim doorway ajar behind me, I am obliged to feel my way, dry fingers whispering against cold brick, feeling the chinks and crumbles. I keep imagining that my face will strike some vast spider web, but it never happens. It seems that, just one turn ahead, down below somewhere, there is a faint light. And yes, as it turns out, another slow downward circle brings me to a door behind which light forms a dull rectangular halo.

Through the door, which I have to shove and scrape, there is a long squat storage room lit by a single torch spitting in the wall near me. It feels drafty. "Hello?" I call. I am answered by echoes. The other walls disappear into shadow, but near me, on a cloth tarp, is a large assemblage of objects so random it takes a while to make them out: andirons, a dry stone fountain, three rubber balls, a shower curtain, a shovel, a cheap wooden stool, all piled together in the center of the tarp. Along the wall there are a few single items that have clear hand-lettered tags. There is, for example, a lush chair that reads:

This is yet another chair. An indolent race, the English are always inventing cunning new ways to sit down. This one was made under King Gregory, and chairs like this are the main reason anyone remembers Gregory at all.

Nearby stands a golf club, bearing a similar note:

The object of the game of "golf" is to knock a small white ball (the "curlew") from a tiny wooden stand called the "tee" or the "snifter," into a hole (the "hobblepop") from very, very far away. Players are given several tries because most of them are old and have bad shoulders. This particular club is called a "mashie" or sometimes a "niblick," which amounts to the same thing. As the names suggest, the whole game is rather silly, and best enjoyed in one's dotage.

A pocket watch:

The English like to keep track of time according to their own common divisions thereof. A functioning watch allows an English man or woman to keep appointments and, more importantly, to make them. Holding this device in one's pocket occasionally provides the illusion that time can be slowed down. It is a complicated invention that is often invoked to defend the existence of God. For more on the concept of "time," see the note on the coffin, farther ahead.

And yes, there in the middle of the clutter is a coffin. No label yet, it seems. As I walk over to examine it, there is a flash of movement that whips my heart (*The dead raised! Mother of mercy!*), but it's a woman bounding out from where she was hiding inside: a different wonder entirely. Short, barely twenty (it appears), with hair shorn like Joan of Arc. She's dressed in the scandalous men's style made famous by George Sand, but a glance at her bosom confirms her sex. She's wearing a nametag that says, of all things, *Niles*.

"Okay," she says. "You found me. Are you looking for your nametag?"

Niles. That's my name. Is there anything she can't steal?

IV: Salome

"I hadn't even noticed it was missing," I say. "I mean, I thought I left it at home, so they made me a replacement."

"Oh good," she says. "Then I can keep this one. Quote, *'Nametags are a means by which the English avoid having to memorize each other's names, leaving more room in their brains for royal scandals and directions to various pubs.'* That's what I'll say. So you don't mind, do you?"

"Who are you?" She's barely over five feet, but her voice is like a pipe organ. Every word seems to be born of great wind pressure.

"I'm Shiva," she says. "The destroyer."

It's a shockingly fictional thing to say. "That's . . . that's ridiculous," I manage, casting back to the images in the Orientalist Collection. "You're not blue. And Shiva has six arms."

She raises her two arms, curling them skyward and then holding them there like a dancer. "You're right," she says. "I need more. How about it? You can be two of them." This stuns me further, and I guess she gets impatient, watching me gape. "Really, my name's Constance." She pauses. "And now that I think about it, that tells you nothing, does it. No wonder you people's nametags leave no room for patronymics."

"Are you a thief?" I say.

"Of course not," she says. "I'm an anthropologist. This is my collection."

"You stole it," I say. "Some of those things are valuable."

"Not to me," she says. "Not that way. Besides, if I can take it, the person who had it didn't deserve to keep it. It's a question of who wants it worst. This is all worth so much more as an educational tool."

She leans forward conspiratorially and play-punches me in the jaw. "Besides," she says, "I don't think you could really stand to destroy all my work. You know what it's like to mount an exhibit." And I know she's right. I can hear my heart beating and I want her to quote more of her tags. Anything could happen down here, I can smell it.

"How did you know that was my nametag?"

"I've been watching you, for one thing. I've been living here for a few days assembling my collection. But also, and you should know this so I'll tell you, I'm a sensitive. I have the gift of second sight."

"You're a spiritualist?"

"Not spiritual. But I can see the future. For example, I know already that this building will one day crumble to ruins and another building will be erected on top of it, and no one will remember your work here. I know that all love stories end in pain—breakups or breakdowns or death, take your pick. And I know that along the way, in the trip between meeting and death, it's the *sensation* of love, the physical act, which is the best and most interesting element. And I know that we're going to have a few adventures together, we'll get along really well, and our trust will slowly build until—bang!—we have sex. Which means, as far as I'm concerned, we may as well have the sex part now."

"I . . . I beg your pardon?" I am swaying a little.

She takes a patient breath. "Look, let's say you're reading a novel. And you wonder whether the Comtesse de Arnise is going to wind up with Baron Oberlin, or run off with the simple but pure-hearted farmhand Lars, or be flattened by a lorry in front of the steps of Saint Anne's Rectory. The fact is, you already know. You hold the answer in your hand. So if you read along in ignorance, you're deliberately fooling yourself. I realize some people find that charming, but I say why bother. Fun parts first is my rule. And what I'm telling you is, why don't we just skip to the sex scene?"

"Oh . . . " It dawns on me slowly, precisely because it's unexpected, but here in this odd little room far beneath the world I know, and with nothing recognizable around me, she sounds like she's making sense. And I haven't actually connected with another person in so long. (It's not against regulations, per se, but the separateness of this place lingers on your clothes into whatever private life you possess.) "Okay, I guess. But I should warn you," I say, "as far as sex, I mean. I'm not very practiced in such things, and . . . and, well, particularly in this . . . in this . . . *circumstance* where I am, you know, surprised, overwhelmed, terribly, terribly nervous . . . "

"Perfect!" she says. "I hate predictable climaxes." And this is how it happens: Constance removes her blouse, indicating with a head-gesture that I am to do the same. She drops her slacks, and before I know it I am folding my uniform and leaving it on a cabinet near a collection of spigots and a garden gnome. I don't know where my sword should go. Her body is warm, very warm, and by the time my back hits the tarp-covered floor I realize that I can be that warm too. I look up at her and I forget where I am, and who is on top, and I operate on some scientific instinct for pleasure where despite my attempts to distance myself everything keeps tipping and turning, and it's all her. Looking at her tiny interesting breasts. Tasting her shoulder (like a wing, I imagine), smelling her, entering,

V: Pearly Eye

but I mostly remember her eyes, eyes the fiercest shade of

VI: Green Comma

green,

VII: Funereal Dusky Wing

and with a tense shift somewhere, I lost whatever stable plans I'd had till then, bucking and thrusting under the shadow of a cross comprised of sticks and twine (*As this exhibit demonstrates, this important English religious symbol is childishly easy to construct . . .*) and an urn of velvet roses (*The skill involved in making velvet flowers is not only material, but is an exercise of the memory, a ritual in which the flower-maker must simulate what flowers look like without actually going outside to check. In England, this is a practice entrusted to women who have no needs.*)

As promised, I climaxed early. She pulled herself off me and slapped me playfully on the belly. "Good work!" she said. "I like how you can mate in captivity. Whew!" I just lay there for a bit, catching my breath and feeling her dampness on me, perversely enjoying the feeling of being cold, spent, and fluid-stained on the floor of an unused cellar. It felt like I hadn't noticed my body in years. Whew was right.

But I also felt distinctly like I'd just been collected, and I didn't like feeling that way, like I was just another bug on her pin. I wanted something back. As she moved around, I watched her, looking, I suppose, for a weakness, for something deeper than her sex. She didn't have any that I could see, except that she seemed young and a little childlike.

"Who are you really?" I said, as she rose to collect her clothing. "You seem like—like you're trying to be above all the rules."

"Oh, God, no," she said. "I'm a slave same as everybody. In fact, before I went on this mission, I made a label for myself." She flipped through her clothing, found it, and tossed it to me: a white card, with her careful handwriting. *The Trickster is a wish fulfillment character in repressed cultures. They look like the people who aren't in power, and are thereby free to say what-*

ever they want. It's a fun way to live, but there are rules, and a happy ending is not guaranteed. One hopes they enjoy themselves before they are punished.

"Did you get to the end?" she said. "The answer is, I just enjoyed myself."

I blushed and cast around for my clothes. That way I could avoid saying something about her dark, troubling nametag. She was still trying it out. It was one thing she was unsure about.

"Oh, look," I said. "There's my sword." In my haste, I'd shoved it under a stand bearing Descartes' death mask, or its impostor.

"Or no," she added, snapping her fingers. "The answer is, I'm an exhibit too. Sometimes we run wild."

"It's not safe, your being here," I said, buckling. "I mean, tonight of all nights."

"Why?" She was almost fully dressed. She was faster at it than I was, like a minuteman.

"The rioters," I said. "The Rabble. We have it on good authority that they may come here any minute. They've already broken every window in the business district, and we know we'll be targeted next. It's inevitable, just like the Louvre during that business in France."

Constance paused. "Do you hear anything? Anything that sounds like yelling or violent looting?" We waited for a few beats.

"Well, no, but—"

"I don't think they're coming," she said.

"Well, if they do, we're ready!" I said. "We have soldiers with halberds all around us. We have boiling oil on the museum roof. We're boarding up windows and doors. If it's a war they want—"

"Oh, come on," she said. "Unclench and help out. I want you to show me what's upstairs."

"Wait!" I said. "You're not a rioter, right? You're not going to steal anything?"

"I'm not a rioter. I'm just an anthropologist. I'm studying museum behavior." She paused and wagged a finger at me. "And misbehavior. I'll be honest. That performance you just gave was so intense it almost made me sad. Has it been a while?"

"I—"

"Actually, I don't want to know. Look, Niles. If the rioters are coming, what difference does it make? You may as well make your last night here interesting. If you won't do it for me, do it for the apocalypse."

I stood there thinking for a bit, one suspender on, shirted and pantsed, but still missing shoes and socks. She made me want to free myself, but she did it by demanding my obedience. I chafed slightly before acceding. "Nothing expensive," I said.

She raised her hand oathwise. "May the king die a virgin."

Already, the eternal timeless presentness of my workplace seemed to be vanishing into a voracious and more powerful past. Even here, under the sconce: a tiny crack. "Fine," I said. "You'll love this place. It's just loaded with crap." I had never said *crap* before. It wasn't like me. Except now it was, forever, or for who knew how long.

VIII: African Map

Our first stop was the map room. "Ooh!" she said. "I love these!"

"There are postcards in that drawer over there," I said. "I can always claim they got lost in the move."

"What move?" she said. She tugged at a drawer and I tossed her the keys.

"The whole thing," I said. "Everything. We've got a new organizing principle. When the Museum started, things were displayed only by type. For example, the Headstone Room—nothing but headstones. Grave markers from China, from Japan, from India, from Africa, all from different time periods and all clustered together in a single room. That was the way we always did stuff: like goes with like. All the arches together. All the butterflies and moths. Swords in one room, armor in another. In a way it makes sense. These things started as private collections, you know."

"Like some people collect stamps," she said, flipping through the cards. "Oh, I don't have this one!" It was a drawing of the Royal Albert Hall.

"But now there's this idea of progress. Darwin, et cetera. And people are expecting us to organize things by timeline, you know, and by continent. So we're breaking up the sets of headstones and putting all the Japanese ones together side by side in chronological order. Then we're lugging the Norse ones into the Northern Europe room. And so on. It's more orderly . . . "

"And educational," said Constance. "Can I take this pen? Thanks."

" . . . But I find it unsettling. It's as if we've still got our old exhibits, but now we're collecting Time and Space on top of them. It feels like something might collapse." I looked at her flipping through cards, fumbling through papers, and suddenly in this light I saw her clearly. "Hey," I said. "Where are you from?"

"All over," she said. "Why?"

"Your skin is brown."

"Tanned, yes. I sail a lot."

"So you're not a . . . not a . . ."

"A what? A product of miscegenation? I don't know actually. Why should you care? Look at this place. Like the collision of cultures surprises you?" She grabbed two maps and slid them roughly together: *whoosh whoosh whoosh.* "Oh no! Look! Antarctica's having sex with Iberia! They'll have really pasty children who squint a lot! Quel horreur!"

"Okay, that's enough!"

"I can't stop them! They're insatiable! Quick! Send them to separate rooms!"

"Constance, you're messing up the maps!"

She stopped and looked at me. "How can anyone tell when a map is messed up? Most of those lines aren't even visible. Where does that door go?" Suddenly pointing.

It was the big side door. "To the entry hall. It's where we keep all the large exhibits."

"Is that the giant whale skeleton with the chairs inside?"

"We call it The Whale Experience, but yes. We just finished it. We were planning to put up the signs tomorrow, but . . . you know. The riots. It's off limits."

"I've never had a whale experience," said Constance, eyes bright. "Let's be the first."

The first. I'd never felt like the first to do anything. In this job, you tend to feel like the owner of a book that's been checked out from the library going back ten thousand years; the last signatory, with nothing new to offer but sober observation.

"Let me check," I said. "There are people wandering all over tonight."

IX: Marine Blue

It was clear. But there were low rumbles—not just from the roof but from distant rooms as boxes shifted, exhibits faced new directions. Our way was now littered with items out of their contexts, relics in uncomfortable abeyance, and I suddenly noticed how much an unmoored museum looks like so much heavy jetsam. How long had I been downstairs?

"This way," I said, leading her around a plaster statue of hawk-headed Horus. Behind us, at least twenty old ploughshares.

The Whale Experience was simplicity itself: our nation's first fully reconstructed blue whale skeleton: sixty-six feet, six inches long from end to end. But to make it an "experiential draw" (The Q's term), Quincunx had assembled a sort of patio inside the whale, with stairs going up to a set of elegant chairs and tables, so you could sit in an open space ten feet off the floor and stare at the museum through the world's largest ribs.

We sat down. The chairs were white wrought-iron patio chairs, more suitable for a view of a garden from some high verandah. The patio itself had an absurdly low interior wall along all four sides, presumably to prevent outside onlookers from seeing up visiting ladies' dresses.

"I feel like Jonah," I said. Then I said it again, daring to speak louder: "I feel like Jonah." An obvious joke, I suppose, but I was the first person to make it from here inside the whale.

"I was going to say Pinocchio," said Constance. "Is there anyone else?"

"Saint Brendan, I think. Maybe Sinbad." I thought then of pepper, how Pinocchio used it to gain freedom, while Jonah simply waited for the next act of God. I was suddenly ashamed at the timidity of my meta-phoric instinct. An urge to do something different struck me and I boldly reversed my chair, looking now away from the museum and out the window. Over the river, out to the city, a glow showed in the distance, brighter than our new electric lights.

"They've set something on fire," I said. "A warehouse, I think. Near the wharf."

She turned her chair around and watched with me. I put my arm on the back of her chair, my hand just brushing her hair. She leaned forward, putting her chin in her hands, resting her elbows far up on her knees.

"Fire's the worst," I said. "It destroys everything. I mean, we're right on the water, so we can put a fire out, but the second it starts, you can't get some things back." I stretched out my fingers, as if I was exercising them, and brushed her back. I could see her backbone sticking up gently between her shoulders. "Your spine," I said, touching it with an index finger. "Someday someone's going to assemble an exhibit around us, and build a little house in your ribcage maybe."

"Sorry, Niles, but we had the climax already, remember? There's no point trying to build anything."

I thought back to the map room. "So why steal? Why label?" She didn't say anything. I pressed her. "You're trying to build something."

"My labeling, this night. This is all a joke," she said. "I'm building a joke." She sounded offended.

"I think you want your own museum," I said. "The only difference between us is that you don't like to share. If this was a zoo you'd be setting the animals free and taking a few home."

She actually said nothing. She just sat there, with my hand on her back, and it was dark, of course, but it looked like she was thinking.

X: Big Greasy

The noise of boot-thuds and the screech of a familiar dragging sword encroached on our hiding place. We ducked from our chairs, hunkering behind the low patio wall. I peeked. It was Muenster, leading a train of three sweaty under-docents, pale, nervous-looking lads of only a few weeks' experience, each one struggling to move an overladen dolly piled with crates, each crate bursting with straw. Plaster models of Roman busts, to judge by crate size and trajectory.

"You know what?" said Muenster, who wasn't carrying anything at all. "Just dump these right here. There's no point moving these things from one room to another if we don't know what room it is or if we'll have to just move it all out again. Leave them here—scattered and cluttered in fact. It'll get in people's way and someone will decide to do something about it." He raised a hand to his eyes, as if he had a headache, and said, "I swear to god, it's like there's no one in charge here. Our leaders have abdicated, and now with the riots . . . " He shook his head. "Jesus, don't just stand there. Unload. We've got to move the Egypt stuff. That's the one thing I'm sure of."

So they unloaded, and we watched in silence, our breath bated so it wouldn't cause undue steam. The crates snaked along the passage, and as the troop marched away I realized the crated artifacts weren't busts at all; they were exhibits from the Cabinet of Oddities, Muenster's favorite. A bottle containing a fetal two-headed calf, a formaldehyded dwarf baby, a Feejee Mermaid and such.

"That was Muenster," I murmured to Constance. "A co-worker of mine. I don't really like him that much." She didn't reply, but it made me feel good just to say it. It struck me that maybe I should tell the truth more often.

XI: Ghost Brimstone

I decided we'd had enough whale. "This way," I said. "It's my favorite room." We crouched and moved along the line of crates.

"Oh, wait! What's this?" said Constance, stopping. Stopping! Right there in the hallway where anyone could see us. What had arrested her attention were a portrait and a jar. The portrait was of Mademoiselle de

Boeuf-Cointreaux, a French noblewoman posed in regal furs and a pompadour, a serious expression on her face. And right over her eyebrows were two tiny horns, like you'd see on a faun. And there, in the jar, were the horns themselves, little thumby nubbins of cutis preserved for aye. They looked like snail shells.

"We got that from a traveling merchant," I said. "She was a real person. There's a card in there somewhere that attests to its authenticity, signed by the Archbishop of somewhere."

"Devil and saint, working together," she said, with the first tone of awe I'd heard in her voice. "Both dead now, I imagine."

"I guess."

"Such a shame." She drew her fingers over the horns in the portrait. "It gives her such a distinctive look, don't you think? I mean, you'd never forget her."

"Had you ever heard of her before?"

"No," she admitted. "But now we've met." Her eyes shone. "Art thee man or art thee beast?"

"Is that a poem?" I asked.

"It is," she said, and touched the jar with the horns. "It really is."

"We've got to move," I said. "People will see us."

"I hope you don't rest," she said, still staring at the picture. "I hope you're haunting the hell out of someone." She kissed her fingers, touched them to the jar, and said, "Okay. I'm ready."

Maybe it was the Whale Experience, that moment I thought we'd had, but I kissed my fingers too, and placed them right where she had. I wasn't sure why. For luck? Because I agreed? To finally touch something in a way I wasn't supposed to? The moment I did, suddenly it was my portrait, and I loved it more than I ever had.

"That's so sweet," said Constance. And she kissed her fingers and touched them to my cheek. "Now we should go."

I nodded, and led the way to the next section. But I could still feel her fingertips on my face. I had just been labeled.

XII: Lost Metalmark

And finally we made it back to the Annex of Miscellany-cum-Egypt Room where I'd started the evening. "This is the butterfly collection," I said. "This one case is only a small sample, of course."

"What's written in the dust there?"

"Up old new low, the ibises don't move."

She turned and looked at them. "Not anymore they don't. So—can we take the top off?"

"I've got keys, of course," I said.

And then, for the first time in my years of docentship, I actually saw all the butterflies without any intervening glass. Doubly amazing, since I'd had the keys all the time. We stood at either end of the case, resting on our elbows and staring at all the colors. When we breathed, the dead wings fluttered.

"That's a viceroy," I told her. "That's a gray hairstreak. That's a blue admiral. They're not all labeled, but I know them. I've always wanted to be like them, you know. Beautiful and free. I suppose that's trite."

"You have a strange definition of free." Constance uprooted a purple morpho, pin and all, moved it toward me about two inches, and then stuck it back in. "Check," she said.

I laughed—laughed, in The Museum!—and moved a yellow fritillary an inch to the left.

She slid a copper diagonally toward me.

I tipped over a metalmark. "Mate," I said.

"If you say so," she replied. "Normally I prefer to mate first and check later." She looked at the glass top. "This is my favorite thing so far, this pane of glass. But it's heavy, so I'm going to just run down and put it with all the other stuff. Then I'll come right back again and we'll look around some more."

"Don't go," I said. "There's nothing there. It's all coffins and bodies."

"Somewhere else then," she said, and picked up her bag with one hand, yanked the glass under her right arm with a grunt. "I'll be right back. I promise. Ta ta." Then she scuttled away.

So I waited for her, and watched the butterflies as I waited. Although I'd long been a fan of this exhibit, until Constance removed the glass, I hadn't really thought about why I loved it so much. It wasn't that the butterflies were pretty—though they certainly were—or that they seemed ineffably fragile—again, undeniable—but the nature of their mounting. No other creatures were pinned, as it were, in mid-flight, so these butterflies, alone among the exhibits, looked as if they'd been literally frozen in time in the middle of their lives, bright verbs be-nouned into submission. This was the only exhibit that gave a hint that these creatures might possess a future. Or would have, under a different sort of curator.

I suddenly had an idea for a label for the coffin downstairs: *"The coffin stores a dead body, and marks the moment when a person stops growing and starts merely accumulating unused time. It is like a very small museum."*

The door opened behind me. I smelled smoke. Had they come at last, and with torches?

XIII: Whirlabout

"Who's there?" I cried, turning.

"Jesus Christ," said Muenster, waving another cheroot from his endless mystery stash. "Where have you been all night? We've got to start on those goddamn sarcophagi, and I'm sure as hell not doing it alone." He strode in, a little wobbly from exhaustion, found Constance's chair and collapsed with a sigh. *An indolent race . . .* I thought. His sword was missing. I didn't ask.

"I've been moving pottery," I said. "I saw you earlier with some of those new kids. They can handle the Egyptians. But it takes a skilled hand to move the fragile stuff like the pottery."

"Or those butterflies," said Muenster, making a halfhearted gesture of accusal with his cheroot hand. "What were you going to do? Take them out one by one? I mean, no offense, Niles, but you're an idiot. Just move the whole fucking case. It's easier."

"We're dividing everything up by region now, remember? It goes for butterflies too. Don't tell me how to do my job. And put out that cigar. I can't believe you're smoking around this stuff."

He looked at me for nineteen long heartbeats, not so much searching my face as attempting to stare it down. Then, without even looking at what he was doing, he licked his fingers, twisted the cigarette out with a hiss, and stood.

"Do what you want," he said. "But Quincunx wants the sarcophagi moved. He didn't say a damn thing about butterflies. There's still a chain of command in this place. We'll be on the big stuff soon. Don't be long."

And he left, rapping his knuckles on the door twice as he exited.

I waited for several more minutes for Constance to return, irritated that Muenster's smoke was dulling the smell of Constance upon me. The moisture from her kiss was already evanescing, I could tell. No wonder she destroyed things. Better than watching them decay and fail by themselves. I waited as long as I dared, maybe five minutes, then decided to step outside into clearer air. Even if I couldn't see her, I thought I might be able to smell her again. They say smell is the sense that is most strongly connected to memory.

XIV: Striped Policeman

As soon as I stepped into the hall, I heard a distant "You there!" Quincunx's voice. I stopped; tether of command.

"Niles," he said. (Clop, clop.) "Go help Muenster. And you can take off your sword. I've just gotten word. The rebellion is over. It never even made it across the river." Sure enough, he was halberdless. Behind him, far down the hall, the guards were returning from the roof, casting off bandoliers and hats.

"What do we do with the oil?" I asked, wondering, even as I asked, why this was the first thing I thought about.

Quincunx shrugged. "Who cares? Give it to the poor, save it up for next time. There's more rebellion where that one came from, I'm bound."

He turned away, then snapped his fingers. "Oh, right." He flipped something through the air at me. I caught it. It was my old nametag.

"Where'd you get this?"

"Got it off a thief we found in the East Gallery. A woman dressed like a man."

"Where is she now?" I asked. My voiced shrilled, and I felt my throat pulse.

He looked baffled. "In custody. Probably in prison already. Don't worry. She wasn't armed. You're safe now." He pointed down the hall toward the Egyptian artifacts and turned with another click of his heels.

Safe, I thought as he walked away, and I pictured a safe closing around me, filled with money that would never be spent. I closed my hand over my cheek again. All curators are sentimentalists. All curators are doomed.

XV: Confused Cloudy Wing

"I'll be right with you," I called after Quincunx. "Let me just . . . " But he wasn't listening and didn't turn, which was just as well. I wasn't sure how to end the sentence.

I felt something smiting my heart. Poor Constance! She of the green eyes, musky scent, dreaming perhaps of real horns. In a prison, now, somewhere safe.

Maybe this is why we have museums: because we can't control anything else. I was reminded of the animists in the Oriental Wing, the ones we ridicule for their belief in totem animals and the wearing of skins. Something primal welled inside me (me on the floor, her atop, sweating beneath that cross, the roses) and I found myself gathering the butterflies, plucking them out, pin and all, one by one, and collecting them in my overcoat, which I cinched tightly and low at the waist, as if I were a shoplifter. There were a hundred and thirty: monarch, viceroy, yellow fairy, metallic blue, green fritillary, long dash. I yanked them free from their moorings, away from their names and dates, and piled them together in a collection I held to my belly. Already they were flaking to dust.

I waddled my way carefully up the stairs beyond the World of Metals, through the second BY PERMISSION ONLY door that led to the roof. The stairwell was narrow, and littered with abandoned halberds and castoff gloves. A clomping from ahead of me turned into a guard—a surprisingly young man, face rosy from the cold, blowing and stamping. "There's no one up there," he said. "No reason to go up." But he didn't stop me, and just passed me by. The last soldier. What if they had a war, but everyone had the time wrong? What if a war actually happened, but it was so quiet and boring no one noticed it?

I pushed up the trap door to the roof, and stood among the pots of oil, all extinguished but still steaming in the night air. It smelled like a giant outdoor kitchen. The pots were modest kettles the size of pigs—I counted twelve, evenly spaced; four along the long sides and three along the short—each of them mounted on a four-legged frame with an axis for easy tipping. The roof was flat and covered with gravel. I scuffled atop everything, thinking.

West, I thought, tasting the wind. The wind is blowing to the west. I bet that's where Constance came from. What else can I do? Who else can I appease? So I went to the western corner of the roof, looking out on the snow-caked river in the distance. I squatted, clutching my bounty, and opened my coat. Then, taking up handfuls of shattered butterflies, I held my hands over the edge and rubbed them together, rolling the dry beetle bodies back and forth, turning them to brightly colored dust that floated away under the moon's ancient light. I did this over and over for what felt like hours until they were all gone and my skin glittered like a mounted trout's. The pins bit blood into my hands, but I knew they'd heal whether I wanted them to or not.

THE LAW

Mariev Finnegan

Jacob hits a button on the Astrovan's radio. Dusty Stump's favorite song, "Life Is a Highway," is playing as we approach the sign that reads: LEAVING THE RESERVATION: *THE ERIE IS COMING.*

On the Rez, where fireworks are legal, Jeff Sky Hawk, an Erie, mixed gunpowder—and nitrates and different compositions to give colors—with Dusty's ashes into assorted fireworks. The flashy red box filled with rockets sits way in the back of the extended Astrovan that contains generations of Erie children. I am driving. I am the Matriarch of the Erie. I connect all Erie.

Everyone is Erie.

Erie mental structuring is not in linear form, but rather holographic: Each contains the whole. And the whole contains each Erie. The *Erie is capable of immediate connection with the sacred: Consciousness unconfined by space. Or time. Or a physical being. Free. The essence of our being is unconditional love. As the Erie say, Love, without reservation.*

Beside me in the passenger seat is Dusty's son, Jacob Stump, age 13. His dark hair covers his face to avoid intimacy. Jacob resembles his father, but he has my blue eyes. My long black hair is streaked white from sorrow; it has never been cut.

Jacob warns me urgently, "You're going too fast, Grandma."

Lightning turns the world brilliant; thunder shakes the earth. The atmosphere is white, then black. We pass over the border of the sovereign nation, where fireworks are legal—then they are not!

Suddenly! At once! Eriemmediately! Sirens and red and white spastic lights like a psychic break in reality. A cop car cuts in front of the Astrovan, shedding waves of discordant light and sound. I brake, both feet on the pedal, but no response. A collision. Like two particles. My oversized van—full of children, a three-legged dog, a white owl and my son's ashes packed into fireworks, like a higher evolutionary form—has run over and now occupies the same space as the tiny cop car.

Superimposed.

The siren is as unrelenting as a pulsating nerve. I view from on high a bar of flashing lights inches from my front window. Dusty's song plays on.

I snap off the radio, and at the same moment, the cop car's siren falls to a low wailing, the flashing lights die.

Every Erie inside the Astrovan is situated in a fixed determination. Still gripping the steering wheel, feet pressed on the brakes, my attention turns to the squished cop car beneath me. The driver's door opens with a grinding of metal, and a little, teeny-tiny, uniformed figure jumps out, making excited noises.

I know this authority figure, badge number 911.

I am Matriarch of the Erie, and 911 is the law.

At some deep level of reality, we influence each other, we are quantumly entangled. We can separate to opposite ends of the universe, the law and I, but any change to 911 effects a complementary change in me. And vice versa.

Because we have need of each other.

911 doesn't recognize me, I can tell. He runs around in crazy circles, screaming God's name, if God had a name, then he jumps up and down as if he imagines me, whoever I am (I could be God) smashed underfoot.

"You ran over my car!"

Synchronization: One last long blast from the siren blends with the cop's despairing wail.

"Whoooo . . . Youuuuu ran over my car. Youuuu almost killed me . . . Yooouuu!"

A bolt of lightning casts stark shadows from the cornstalks lining each side of the road; I have a feeling of being enclosed by skeleton fingers. 911 approaches, one hand on his holstered gun. He manages to get the formalities out—"License, registration and insurance"—and adds as an afterthought to himself, "A Rez-Runner." He nods. Smiles. 911 figures I have no license; certainly no insurance.

Erie possess an unusual pair of psychological attributes: Intense psychic abilities and a disposition for difficulty with authority.

In the mirror, I see behind me the sign that marks the imaginary line between the law and the Rez. Holding 911's shaded eyes in a direct stare, I shift the Astrovan into reverse, step hard on the gas. No response, except the tires spin in air. 911 is pulling an object that looks like an inhaler from his front pocket. He points it directly at my face. It is pepper spray. His finger is on the trigger of the canister. I brake and put the transmission into neutral.

The owl feathers I wear in my black hair stand at alert. I hold one palm out flat toward 911. "How."

"How fast were you going?" There is an hysterical edge to his voice. His eyes are 3-D behind his dark glasses. He is seeing too much. Too soon.

"Faster than the speed of light," I guess.

I do a hit on my hand-rolled cigarette. I am high. I blow my inhaled smoke toward the tiny, little, little man's face, so he can be high, too. Then I swallow the end of my doobie. The evidence.

911's black eyes study Jacob in the passenger seat. Some eerie energy passes between them. Jacob asks, "Don't you recognize me?"

"Are you wanted?" 911 asks suspiciously.

I shudder, as if someone just walked over my grave. "That proposition may be both true and untrue at once."

A light appears phenomenologically in the sky. Thunder whacks. There is a brilliant stroke of lightning, and in its glare I see a white white phantom.

"I'm missing time," Jacob moans.

I point at the light making maneuvers in the air so sharp they would kill a human pilot. "A UFO."

911 doesn't see it, doesn't even turn his head to look.

"I'm in a quantum non-locality," Jacob says. "I'm abducted!"

"Kidnapped?" 911 asks, his suspicion accelerating.

Jacob stares beyond 911: "I'm in two places at once, of my own free will."

911 pockets the pepper spray and reaches for his Taser.

He points it at Jacob. "Do you need help?"

Silence. A pause.

911 cranes his neck to look past me into the back of the Astrovan. Thunder follows lightning, and the van rolls back a few inches. Cubed.

"None of those kids are seat-belted!" 911 is outraged, scanning the interior of my van filled with generations of children. I've never counted the children, I am uncertain how many are now inside the Astrovan, yelling, jumping around like buckyballs. (Buckyballs defy gravity—I collect them.)

"And that dog! Are you aware of the new law?" 911 points with the Taser at Bloody Stump, the three-legged dog, who returns the look with his different colored eyes.

Now the earth moves with a roll of thunder. I call out to 911, "The Erie is coming!"

A flash of lightning equal to the thunder.

911 roars: "It's illegal to transport animals unless they are caged or otherwise confined!"

In a world full of light from everywhere at once, Bloody Stump leaps through space toward the open window. 911 pulls the trigger on the Taser. Electrified currents, cruel fingers of fate, dance in air.

I catch Bloody in my arms, his muscular body still in motion, and calm him by scratching the place behind his right ear he can't reach, because he's missing that hind leg. I scratch with my left hand, the pointer finger missing on my right.

911 reacts to the impotence of his Taser by running around to the back of the extended Astrovan. He has to jump to unlatch the double doors. I see the little officer in the mirror, and the mirror is high and reversed.

He examines my cargo. He whistles and says to himself, "Call in the K-9s."

Then, Eriemmediately, 911 is right up close to explain, as he points the stun gun at me, eye-level.

"The law is that an Indian can only buy untaxed cartons of cigarettes on the Rez for your own *personal* use. Looks like you are *dealing*."

Both my hands up now, palms forward, my gesture: *How* and *Why*. "Those are not cigarettes . . . "

"I knew it!" 911 erupts in vibrations. "It's marijuana."

For one brief moment my eyes connect with 911's. "It is bricks of fireworks. Rockets and missiles containing the ashes of my dead son."

"That's against the law too!"

911 commands me—the Matriarch of the Erie, who connects all Erie, and everyone is Erie—to step out of the vehicle. "I'm searching this Astrovan."

"Not without a warrant," I say wisely.

Allisha, who is bad, but will never be as bad as Grandma, jumps forward from the back seat. She leans both pudgy hands on my right shoulder, her extra-large curly head next to mine. Allisha spits a big green glutinous gob in the face of 911.

One kid, I suspect it is Junior, throws a string of lit firecrackers at the little law man.

911 screams, "I'm calling for backup," then freezes.

Then 911 raises his Saigon sunglasses and rests them on his head of short spiked hair. He takes a good look at me with his black eyes.

"You." The word is ripped from him. "You!"

He recognizes me!

He takes a sudden involuntary breath, and the word comes out long like his breath: "*You.*"

911 pulls his gun and points it at my heart. "I know you. I know who you think you are."

"I'm the Matriarch of the Erie." I use a soothing voice.

"Erie-extraterrestrial," 911 shoots back. His eyes bulge and turn red like an animal that can see in the dark. 911 puts the barrel of his gun to the center of my forehead. Then he notices the white owl way in the back of the cargo area. "There is an owl in your van," he squeaks in disbelief. My totem, Who? becomes agitated.

"You . . . *You!* It is illegal to own an owl. You must have a permit to confine anything wild."

Who? flies right over me and out the window. Who? circles 911's head, then flies off into the lightning. Who? crosses the imaginary line to the Rez. Who? is free.

"Your mother is dead," I cry out to 911, or Dusty Stump as he is called by the Erie. "I see her. She is right behind you!"

911 cocks the gun pressed against my third eye. "What does she look like?"

"She looks like me."

A silence.

"I'm Matriarch of the Erie, Dusty." 911 looms, his physical presence takes up much space. Suddenly he's large, intimidating.

"Erie behave as both waves and particles," I remind him. "We Erie are able to instantaneously communicate with each other regardless of distance or vibration or time or death. Any change to one Erie effects a complementary change in all the others. It happens Eriemmediately." I search his face. "The Erie are coming. We are all Erie. Everyone is Erie!" I sob.

His dark eyes, bloodshot and weeping, roll in his head, then center on my blue eyes. 911's finger tightens on the trigger. "I'm not. I'm *not* Erie."

There is a crash of thunder like warfare, then a flash of white, white light that is at once Eriewhere. Erienergy splashes from an open vein in the sky. Flickering coils blind me like the aftermath of a gigantic camera flash, and the air itself becomes a negative. For long seconds, Dusty is embedded on my retinas.

What happened? Cause? Effect! There are as many possibilities as there are universes and Erie.

One possibility: 911 pulled the trigger. The bullet from his gun set off the fireworks, an explosion of rockets containing his ashes. Climactic event. Big Bang!

Another possibility: Organismic lightning rearranged all the bucky-balls and Erie to balance in multiple states, existing at the same time, in-definite until measured in both position and movement. Nothing exists until it is observed. That's called Eriexistentialism.

Certainly, a faster-than-light information exchange occurred, and an entangled pair was observed. The law took on a definite value (e.g., clockwise spin), and the Erie took the complementary value (e.g., coun-terclockwise spin).

We were an entangled pair. Now, it seems, we have been separated.

Matter and antimatter cannot coexist. Antiparticles annihilate each other.

That is the law.

—◊◊◊—

At the same time, *Eriemmediately,* there is a brilliant stroke of lightning, its blinding glare followed by the loud reports of multiple explosions, vibrations shaking the earth.

Five hundred feet up, lights zinging in, inzaning out. The Erie is coming.

Erieverything is seized in a brilliant light, shining from a buckyball in spectacular upward flight. I'm screaming across space! Space is what we all, even the Erie, fear.

From on high, in cosmoagony, I explode in space. Numerous shells boom and whistle. My son's ashes, 911/Dusty, me, the Erie are released in whirling eruptions of metallic flames and cascading meteor show-ers. And every rocket lets off smaller explosions: whirligigs, geometric forms, waterfalls, tree pieces and lattice work. The insane pyrotechnic spectacle is directly above the border that defines the law.

Some of 911's ashes are legal, but some are not.

The Erie have come.

—◊◊◊—

I'm actualized, not in a direction but a dimension, across the imaginary line. I'm on the Rez, where there is no law. High in the driver's seat of the Astrovan, I now face the sign: LEAVING THE RESERVATION: *THE ERIE IS COMING!*

I am myself, Matriarch of the Erie, in the driver's seat of the Astrovan, facing the border, where now I see a straight road, nothing in my way. The storm front passes overhead to expose the full moon, a perfectly balanced ball in space. I'm drained, but I'm not as uncertain as I used to be.

Who? flies in the window to perch on my shoulder, as the last of the ashes fall around us. Jacob hits a button on the radio. "Life Is a Highway," Dusty's favorite song, is playing.

I step hard on the gas.

THE HARD PROBLEM

Rachel Yoder

Okay. Let's just calm down. Let's just approach this rationally. There's no need to go getting all belligerent. There's no need to invoke "unicorns" and "death" and "boobs." There is a need for precision and measured thought. There is a need for NO EMOTIONS and the absence of FREAKING OUT and only for a very serene sciencing.

Science says that the hard problem comes in trying to explain consciousness. The scientists get all fussy and fidgety, as if every single one of them is wearing woolen underpants, when they try to articulate what consciousness is. Certainly, according to science, our human experience should be able to be explained as a complex system of firing neurons and chemicals and blood runnething through our unholy veins, but the hard problem for the itchy scientists comes after all the neural paths are charted, after every chemical is taxonomized and neatly labeled in block print, after every last drop of blood has been accounted for. The hard problem exists on the other side of answers, in the quiet valley where the itchy scientists receive the hard problem mimeographed on a single white sheet.

> Q: What is it like to be an alive human having these insanely
> beautiful experiences of walking through the world? Please
> only use integers in your answer.

The scientists scratch themselves raw. There is talk of "eczema" and "flaking." There are very many soothing tubes of creams. All the equations and maths and very complicated computations might not explain it, might not fully articulate how fucking awesome it is to exist. If the physical data cannot perfectly describe the consciousness of the human animal, then what can? Something "metaphysical"? Something "spiritual" or "new age" or "woo woo"? The scientists scratch and scratch and scratch, through their skin and into the warm blood of muscle. They sink into the throbbing of organs, down to the bones where they whittle away to the marrow and then, finding nothing, start on their heads, scratching off their hair and encountering the skull, boring holes and cracking themselves open, burrowing down through the grayness until all that remains of each of them is a single finger poking at an almost indecipherable wisp of somethingness. This wisp, you see, is the unspeakable integer, uncovered there in the green green valley of silence where seventeen disembodied fingers float in the air, each pointing to its own answer.

And so goes the itchiest problem in the history of the universe.

The writer's hard problem is similar to the itchy scientist's, except the writer is not itchy. She is overflowing with ennui. Perhaps we might say she's "watery." Consider every silence between every word ever written a dark drop in a vast ocean. Consider how many quiet oceans we've filled with our tomes of words and how those seas of silence are where we now swim, struggling for shore. The watery writer writes and writes and writes, a lifetime of words she writes, and still they cannot begin to articulate the love that has wound its way inside her, slowly over centuries, the cool clear water working quietly, indecipherably, until there is a shallow creek bed cut there in the bones. This is her love that has worn away such hardness after millions, after billions, of years. But there is no way to say this, no way to truly write it, to telegraph the bright life, the glare of it, how it hurts and how it's beautiful, how the lifeness of everything grows loud like a great metal ship blaring its foghorn as it infinitesimally moves toward land. There is a ship-shaped meteor approaching. There is a meteor-shaped ship. We should be living as if at every moment the bigness is bearing down on us in a deafening and blinding and overwhelming-in-every-way whoosh but shit and fuck and shit: there is no way of saying this.

There is no way of saying: life.

There is no way of saying: cataclysm.

There is only profanity. There are only water metaphors, and images of vast black oceans. There is only a great white ship with colonies of seaweed-stained barnacles clinging to the hull. There are only meteors that look like cheese or deep sea sponges or the squishy brain of God. There are only space rocks shifting around out there, hopeless.

And what of us, of our hard problem? Forget the scientists. Forget space. I mean, who are you? I mean, tell me what your version of being alive is. For the rest of our days, you'll work on an equation, or a serum, or a very complicated computer program, and I'll sit here at my desk, writing. When we're old and gray, with very many grandkittens and great-grandkittens, we'll exchange projects in an effort to understand the other's reality.

You will have made me a robot that perfectly duplicates the you I fell in love with, back in our younger days. I will have written you a fat book full of thinly-veiled, cat-laced stories chronicling the previous 65 years.

I will connect electrodes to my head and the robot will control me with the powers of its mind. You'll read my book and slowly absorb my style and then, on the day you finish the book, you will take up the pen and continue on where I left off. Eventually, I will happily play video games whilst you labor at your desk, depressed. We won't even know what happened, only that the other person seems so familiar, as if we knew them in a past life. I will watch you and remember what it was like to be me. You will watch me and remember yourself. And eventually, in the end, I hope it's no longer clear which life we lived, nor what we felt. I just want to show you something. I mean, everything.

TWO FULL MOONS AND ONE EMPTY MOON AGO

Steve Castro

I dreamt that I spoke Chinese, but I spoke
Mandarin, and since my dream took me to

Hong Kong,
I was screwed,
Because I did not
Speak Cantonese.

I looked left and saw an old man
Two hundred meters away yelling in
Spanish and holding a brilliant red lobster the size of
My hunger over his head with both hands.

When I approached the Spaniard holding the lobster
I realized that it was Salvador Dalí—Dalí looked at me and said
"I decided to paint the red lobster red: red over red, what do
You think of the use of a crustacean as a canvas?"—
"I saw a large collection of your sculptures at the
Ralli Museum in Caesarea, and if I didn't already know that you died
In 1989, I would ask for your autograph."
Dalí wept.

I waited for the famed artist to regain his composure until
I was distracted by a white mouse that I followed until it led me
To a clown with a smile on his throat who was bleeding
Happy thoughts on the pavement next to
The only cubist lamppost in the world.

I searched his pockets and found a stamped
Envelope—I took out a pen and paper then I wrote a

Menacing letter to my psyche: "Wake me the fuck up or else."
I sealed the stamped envelope & addressed it to myself.
Within minutes a loud noise in the form of a

Telephone ringing awoke me—It was my other self.
"I received a really strange letter, we need to talk.

Meet me at the airport—I will explain everything to you once we land
    in Poland."

WHAT DEATH TELLS US

Soren Gauger

It sometimes happens that the eye of the weary traveler headed north on the Kielce-Skarzysko stretch of highway might, even involuntarily, drift past the double steel road guards and—albeit only momentarily—gaze through the wire fence to spot a decorative gravestone amid the birches, pines, and Lord-knows-what-else. The mental image is so fleeting that only fifteen minutes later a murky montage of impressions emerges from the subconscious:

> a deer dashes into sight,
> > pale in the headlights,
> > > a confusion, a contusion,
> > > > a transfusion

. . . and so on. Though truth be known, the driver can no longer recall the source of these macabre specters, and swiftly rights his train of thought onto more amiable subjects. Meanwhile, if through some enchantment we were able to remove all the obstacles for just a moment, allowing us to approach the gravestone, we would happen upon a curious sight. Carved into the stone, altogether a delightful piece of masonry—a counterpoint of sorts to the foul mess of rotting muscles, cracked skull, and worms of all description just below the surface—instead of the obligatory "He sleeps with the angels," we would find a cautionary verse that says the following:

> Of the horrors of Nature any child could tell
> But the darkest depths most certainly dwell
> In the hearts of other men;
> And the workings of one's very own mind
> You'll certainly find
> Are twice as demonic again.

Beneath which, we find the inscription:

[illegible] Balczyński

1859–1898†

The door flies open with a clatter and we find ourselves standing before [illegible] Balczyński, no longer in the prime of his youth, though not utterly devoid of the charms of an old man-about-town—his moustache has delicately grayed around the corners of his mouth, his eye sockets are perhaps a tad more sunken than he might have wished, and his stride, once sprightly and self-confident, now betrays a certain insecurity. In the company of men he can be witty and impetuous, he easily succumbs to the charms of gambling and a strong *apéritif,* while among women he becomes downright impulsive, infamous for his sudden bursts of temper and impatience.

He is now striding to the dining room for some breakfast, he sits by the table and carefully raises a steaming forkful of scrambled eggs to his lips, while we, in the meantime, bide our time in the corridor of his manor, where we survey the old, second-rate Chinese vases, keepsake photographs, and paintings in gilded frames. Let us pause for a moment in front of a photograph of Balczyński in a white smock. Here we see young Balczyński as a veterinarian. In his arms he cuddles a tan puppy, and in his eyes . . . something is less than clear, though we hesitate to say if the fault lies in the age of the photograph, or if rather the fogginess derives from the subject's intuitive sense of restraint. For who among us could say with any sincerity that he could recall having seen Balczyński's face wear an expression?

With the possible exception of revulsion. Ten years of working as a veterinarian had effectively rid him of any sympathy for the so-called natural world, through daily contact with an indescribably vast repertoire of repulsive specimens. Dogs with distemper and their diarrhea, bloody leukorrhea, vomiting spells, and blisters on their bellies were his frequent guests. Sometimes the dogs had attacks of the furies. The horses with mud fever were no less revolting—their puss-filled, mud-caked sores could be so thick that they had to be scraped off with a chisel. Then there were the rarer cases—cats possessed by some sort of sexual hysteria, birds recalling the deranged scribble of a child with a blunt pencil and a red crayon, pigs with lumps on their bodies that none of the veterinary textbooks described . . . A shotgun hung in the backroom for the worst cases—every veterinarian had one on hand—but he increasingly saw it as an ultimate recourse for himself, disgusted with all manifestations of so-called natural life. And increasingly this "ultimate" recourse seemed all too necessary. Thus he decided to close his office, before his reasons for going on dissipated entirely.

Three years back he had shut the doors of his office for good, exhausted with the nightmares that invariably haunted him with insects of every description, with the knife that was always too blunt to slice open the furry skin. The entire world of beasts seemed to gather ominously around his bedside, baring their teeth, scraping their claws. And yet this business with animals was—how to phrase it?—not entirely resolved.

For it was now—returning to our protagonist where we left him, lifting his forkful of scrambled egg, which has been growing cold during our digression—that is, when Balczyński heard, amidst the clatter of his silver cutlery, the last moans of the cattle in his slaughterhouse, which he had established after closing his veterinary office, on the grounds of his properties—that he had a creeping sense of something like *contentment*. He now accepted his role *vis-a-vis* the natural world and he knew how to move about in it, like switching to a suit that no longer pinched at his armpits, that liberated him.

And yet if we agree that in general the fate of man in the world is a fragile one, then all the more fragile was the fate of Balczyński. At the moment when we rejoin him—the mass of egg still suspended between lips and plate trembling precariously—he has just become aware that a disquieting silence has taken hold in the barn, as if the cattle were suddenly alarmed by something. Balczyński dropped his fork on the plate, splattering the table with scrambled egg, and approached the window to investigate. It was then that he saw his cows in a catastrophic state— some lay on their sides, opening their mouths like fish tossed onto the shore; others just barely stood upright, wobbling drunkenly and bugging out their eyes. The pale sunlight only enhanced the depressing tableau.

Sylwester! he cried for his butler, but for minutes on end no one answered. And thus *Sylwester!* he cried once more, now becoming a trifle impatient, and this time Sylwester appeared in the dining room, but then immediately toppled over, first onto his knees, and then, after a moment's reflection, as it were, onto his face. His complexion was gray, he was winded, his general appearance was diseased.

Without a second's hesitation, Balczyński reached into the cardboard box where he kept all the props of his former occupation, digging out the rubber gloves and the surgical mask. The butler was scarcely able to catch his breath, and prizing open the maw with his fingers Balczyński found a bloody pulp—the patient had already managed to bite through his tongue. Delicately closing his mouth, Balczyński repeated *Sylwester*—this time in a whisper—and then dragged his body to the neighboring room, shutting the door tight behind him.

The next picture hanging in Balczyński's corridor depicted the ruins of a fifteenth-century castle overlooking a lake, apparently a jumble of architectural periods and whims. Looking at it, inevitable associations foisted themselves upon you: wasted potential, or the unsightly remains after the erosion of the brain. In the water's reflection the thing looked more dreadful still—the few remaining legible fragments of its architecture became an utter blur on the surface of the water; history, human aspirations, humor and tragedy, dignity and idiocy became no more than a meaningless smear. It was precisely this picture that Balczyński now passed, beetling his brow and staring into the abyss of financial catastrophe—not a single one of his cows remained alive.

Let us now introduce his neighbor.

Balczyński had only one neighbor, one Ksawery Bundt, an elderly gentleman, also living alone in the sizeable manor just visible from Balczyński's properties. Neither of the men quite recalled who had first set up residence there—if first it was Bundt, and only then Balczyński, or on the contrary, first Balczyński and then Bundt moved in. They kept a tacit agreement to limit their mutual contact to an absolute minimum. But after all—what might they have discussed? Bundt was a bibliophile, he collected books as precious objects, and if he paged through them from time to time, it was only in order to assess their material properties: i.e., the slow erosion of the paper from white to yellowish-brown, the fraying of the corners of the covers, etc. Like most bibliophiles, he had long, spidery fingers, tended to clear his throat too frequently, and was incapable of discriminating between tiresome pedantry and apt observations. He had even less patience for cows' intestines than for the contents of books, and so he kept a safe distance from Balczyński, whom he considered, at any rate, to be dangerous and unpredictable.

Here our chronology falls apart somewhat. We cannot be certain if Balczyński began to observe Bundt by night *before* the massacre of the cows occurred, or only after their death. We have only facts, free-floating in mid-air. Namely: Balczyński observed Bundt every night when the latter would walk over to the old oak tree on the boundary between their properties, carrying a shovel and a lantern. And there under the oak he dug—sometimes for thirty minutes, sometimes almost an hour—until he succumbed to fatigue and returned home. The hole he dug was not visible from Balczyński's window, but it must have been deep indeed, to judge by the quantity of time Bundt devoted to it. At one point, after a number of trips to the oak, Balczyński arrived at the conviction that Bundt most certainly intended to hide a treasure there.

One thought led to the next like beads on a rosary. Bundt was surely digging a place to hide a treasure. My entire herd of cows has just died. The future holds inevitable poverty and humiliation. That miser has no idea what it means to *go hungry*. And the treasure is there precisely between our properties. Bundt is weak and he lives alone. I could steal his treasure before he knew what hit him. If Bundt notices my going there during the night, if he suddenly appears while I'm searching for his treasure, it would be a simple matter to kill him, and without the discomfort of witnesses. And thus the rosary ended in a cross.

A certain brand of psychological narrative would delve here into the sources of Balczyński's readiness to commit a murder. We are ashamed to confess that we, too, had prepared a slapdash justification for this final conclusion, in the form of some dim trauma experienced by Balczyński at a tender age. Ultimately, however, we would ask you to recall that this is a work of history, which, like the photograph, does not trouble itself with commentary, it merely presents the bald facts for the betterment of the reader. If it affects the mind or the soul—indeed, if it affects *at all*—it is only in an oblique fashion.

Balczyński's days were occupied with cleaning bovine corpses. A lugubrious sort of work, rotten to the core and unimaginably lonely. In dragging those bodies, which had meanwhile grown flaccid and limp, his thoughts darted about. Suddenly he had a series of flashes, recollections of his own degradation: the failed attempt to ask one Elżbieta Mańkowska—a woman of Rubenesque charms, the daughter of a renowned industrialist—out on the town, bringing along fifty red roses to sweeten the pot, and the nauseating fragrance of the same flowers that accompanied him all the way home. The mustachioed face of his psychologist saying that if he refused to believe that his deeds had consequences in reality then people would always hold him in contempt. The words *old craphead* scrawled in mud by the local children on the wall of his house, traces of which still remained visible in spite of his (late) butler's repeated efforts to wipe it clean. The blow square in the nose in a pub, in the presence of (ex) acquaintances, which was delivered by a drunken notary who claimed that Balczyński had had improper relations with his wife (this is not accurate: Balczyński had met neither the notary nor his wife), one result of which being the pub owner's subsequent undisguised revulsion at the very sight of Balczyński. The purchase of a very costly picture drawn by Heinrich Dürder, a highly praised German artist of the eighteenth century, from a friendly gentleman with trustworthy eyes and a firm handshake. The discovery, some time later, that such an artist had never existed, and that the unscrupulous traveling salesman had somehow absconded. His father's favorite saying, that in fact he only came to understand the true misery of existence after his only son was born. The moment of clarity he experienced as an eighteen-year-old lad, perceiving that his fully-grown face was not a particularly attractive one; and when he acknowledged the depressing fact, which struck him in a flash, that as a man without good looks and charisma in the years to come he could only anticipate a lack of those pleasures and comforts that others more handsome and charming had handed to them on a plate, that people would be more cruel and ruthless toward him as a result of his physical defects.

And now to top it all off, these dead cows.

Finally came the night when Bundt hauled over his loot and buried it in the hole, spending several hours packing the earth down on top of it. Though fired with enthusiasm at the promise of the treasure, Balczyński felt that now was the time for restraint, for waiting a few days at least, until Bundt's mind began to wander from the business.

Meanwhile, Balczyński was unable to sleep, and for several reasons. Primarily this was the stench of the rotting cows. But furthermore—he was no long master of his own thoughts, his brain independently began imagining the appearance and estimating the value of the treasure, and sketching out his life after he had it in his hands. No less overwhelming was the vague, though firm conviction that the treasure was tied to some form of catastrophe.

Three sleepless nights later, he finally understood that he would go mad if he did not make a swift decision. Under the cover of darkness he made for the old oak with shovel in hand. The silence was compelling. He stole a glance at Bundt's manor—all the windows were dark. The digging began.

What Bundt had buried over the course of several nights Balczyński managed to unearth in five feverish hours. His movements were both violent and mechanical, he kept striking his foot with the spade, but he stubbornly plowed on, scarcely conscious of the time and of his own actions. The harder he panted, the less he registered his own breathing. His pulse thundered.

By the time he had pulled a chest from the hole, a light rain had begun to dapple the collar of his coat. Unable to restrain himself, he went to open the chest at once, but found it closed with a padlock. He hammered at it repeatedly with his spade, in vain. Ultimately he rammed the spade through the lid of the chest, spraining his arm.

Then he reached his hand into the dark depths of the chest and pulled out a canvas sack. At the limits of his patience, he lit the lantern and pulled from the sack a human head. And then, as if on command, his hand still holding the head, he instinctively turned toward Bundt's manor, to see the silhouette of his neighbor in the illuminated window. The pulse of time syncopated strangely. And then the light in the manor window snapped off.

No longer in control of his movements, Balczyński gave the chest a kick, bruising himself in the process, bellowed from the depths of his throat, and then, with what remained of his strength, pushed the foul thing back into the hole. The chest performed a *salto* as it fell in, and its contents could be heard spilling everywhere. The rain picked up, the ground grew spongy. Balczyński tossed the lantern and shovel into the hole and then bolted off through the field, slipping and falling in the mud.

The next picture decorating Balczyński's corridor is a view of a window with a view on an idyllic meadow. In the center stands a deer under a tree, staring inquisitively at the viewer. In the sky: a semi-transparent cloud seems to slowly dissipate before our very eyes. The grass is soft and plush; one senses that lying in it would not prickle. Hard to say precisely if the gentle breeze we feel on our skin in fact is blowing through the corridor, or is the synesthetic influence of the picture on our imagination. Or perhaps mere goose bumps? And now we turn our attention to the space beyond the window frame enclosing the meadow, i.e., to the strips of wall surrounding it, themselves surrounded by the frame of the picture; we see that the wall is scratched, covered in a network of cracks, painted in sickly tones, from a meaty pink to the yellow of a cholera victim's face. We ask ourselves: why is it that the charming scene *within* the frame never brightens the gloom of the outside? Why must it be that the frame inclines us to take a dismal view of what lies within? As if, in the final analysis, the central idyll hid some sort of perversion, some unspeakable horror?

Close your eyes.

We return to Balczyński—while the picture was distracting our attention, it seems that Balczyński has lost something (The key to his manor? A ring? Something else?), and now we find him on all fours, not far from where he would fall once more in the mud, groping all around him, utterly crumpled by the rain and exhausted, when suddenly! the crack of a rifle rings out.

More accurately: Balczyński heard the crack. And moments later, he heard the rabid yelps of Bundt's hunting dogs. Of course, we might easily prefer to mock our protagonist, belittle him—the rifle crack was thunder, naturally, and the dogs most probably the wind howling in his ears. But where, then, do we finish up? Do we intend to prove that the severed head was no more than a clump of hay? That the butler is alive and well? Perhaps even that all of Balczyński's property is a kind of insubstantial pre-war fairy tale that might be dissolved with a wave of the hand, like a puff of steam?

And so our Balczyński was running through the field to the forest, his heart hammering the *Bolero* in his rib cage, until he arrived where we first found him—or his grave, rather—glimpsed through the windshield of a car traveling on sparkling asphalt in our distant twenty-first century, stifling a yawn and staring indifferently at the billboards ("With our cameras—you've got your eye on everything.") constantly flashing by. And if the truth be told: whether that hole in Balczyński's skull was made because he fell in a fit of madness and smashed his head on a rock, or because Bundt appeared and his aim was true—this for us is a purely rhetorical question.

ALPHABET OF THE CELLO

An imaginary colophon

Norman Lock

Loom whose shuttle is a bow weaving watered silks of sorrow and desire, the tomb of silence, shape of woman, of pear, and of a cosmos such as Kepler might have dreamed in Rudolf's palace on the River Jizerou—the cello blinded Jan Novák to all other forms but its. His mind had not succumbed to the music of a string quartet playing *passionato*, but to a perturbation of light on the shoulders of a solitary instrument glimpsed as he entered a room in Prague's Conservatory to glaze a broken pane. For the remainder of his days, he reproduced that exemplary figuration (helpless to resist so suave a persuasion) on paper, misted windows, in snow or dust. His stone in Olšany Cemetery bears no other mark save this, as if the name by which the world knew him were superfluous in eternity.

minnows

Jønathan Lyons

fishie 1.1 "Fed your fish yet?" our mother asks. I say I will. Blue follows after me like a stink I can't scrub off. I pick up the little container full of flakes and Blue says, "How much do we give 'em?"

"A pinch," I say.

"How much is that?"

"What? It's a pinch."

"A big pinch or a little pinch?"

"Jeez, Blue, I don't know."

Blue is quiet for a few seconds, so I pinch a pinch of fish food and throw it on the top of the water.

"What's fish food taste like?" he asks.

2.1 We're family, and families solve their own problems.

0.11 Our mother is awake, but her eyes are dark all around and the skin there wrinkles dry in a web of wrinkles. I tell her I'll make mac and cheese for dinner later and she tells us to sit down.

minnows 1.1 Pop-Pop comes home from work with two smallish gold-fish in a baggie full of cloudy water. "Pets for my boys!" he yells, "My lit-tle men! You two get to name 'em." Pop-Pop goes to the back porch and fishes out a glass tank I always knew was there but didn't know was for fish. He takes it out the back door and hoses it out out back, then brings it back in and sets it on the little table in the dining room. He gives my brother and me each a pan and says, "Fill 'er up!"

5.1 Later, I make our last box of mac and cheese and some powdered milk. There's still a little powdered milk left after. July is burning out from under us and our Pop-Pop is gone and I can't make our mother listen. I leave a bowl of mac and cheese outside her door, but know that in the morning it will be un-ate.

In the morning, the bowl of mac and cheese is right where I left it. Our mother hasn't touched it and she still isn't getting out of bed.

1.1a In the night, I dream of Pop-Pop attacking the house, smashing in all of the ground-floor windows and yelling our mother's name.

4.1 In the morning I wake up to someone knocking on the front door. Outside is my Uncle Jim. He smiles and says "Mornin'. Your Pop-Pop here?"

"No," I tell him. "My mother says he might not come back."

"Where's your phone?"

"We don't have to tell anyone," I say.

3.1 In the morning I wake up to someone knocking on the front door. Outside, Gwen-Doe-Lyne and a cop car have pulled up.

Our mother is shaking.

"What'd you do to our mother?" I say.

She says, "I didn't do nothing. Your pop happened to her."

Our mother is silent and shaking. The cop is actually helping her up the front steps.

2.2 We're family, and families solve their own problems. **We police our own. It's no one else's business.**

0.10 Our mother is awake, but her eyes are dark all around and the skin there wrinkles dry in a web of wrinkles. I tell her I'll make mac and cheese for dinner later and she tells us to sit down. **"Your Pop-Pop isn't probably coming back,"** she tells us.

I say, "What?"

"Your Pop-Pop," she says, and she shakes when she breathes, **"isn't probably coming back."**

minnows 1.2 Pop-Pop comes home from work with two smallish gold-fish in a baggie full of cloudy water. "Pets for my boys!" he yells, "My lit-tle men! You two get to name 'em." Pop-Pop goes to the back porch and fishes out a glass tank I always knew was there but didn't know was for fish. He takes it out the back door and hoses it out out back, then brings it back in and sets it on the little table in the dining room. He gives my brother and me each a pan and says, "Fill 'er up!"

We do. Pop-Pop puts some drops in the tank and we float the baggie in there a while, then let out the fish. "Goldfish?" I say. "Dime feeders," he says to me.

Interstitial 1.1 It's even hotter today, and getting worse and the air heavier.

Hotter and hotter, it's getting late in June and our mother and Pop-Pop fight harder and drink harder against the heat. They go to bed yelling and wake up in sweat.

Our mother tries to run a good house, keep a good home, she tells us that and she makes us dust and do dishes and pick up to show us how it's done right. Dinner, our mother always tells us, is a sit-down meal at the table at 5:30 sharp. Last time I stayed out of sight behind her garden and pretended I didn't hear her call-ing, she put me in bed—*hungry!*—at seven o'clock! I just laid there, bored and hungry.

A Friday and hotter and the musty-wet air all over us, and our mother is in the kitchen making pork cutlets and hamburger helper and cut canned corn. She runs a good house and she keeps a good home. And dinner is at 5:30. And when it's 102 degrees out and the blacktop melts between your toes until your feet are too hot to stay standing on it, and the hot comes up in waves that make the air move like water, and Pop-Pop hasn't made it home by 5:15 to get cleaned up for a sit-down

1.1b In the night, I dream of Pop-Pop at-tacking the house, smashing in all of the ground-floor windows and yelling our mother's name. **Gwen-Doe-Lyne is Our Mother's friend. She's still around, and that seems to make him angrier, 'cause she's an outsider. She don't under-stand.**

0.9 Our mother is awake, but her eyes are dark all around and the skin there wrinkles dry in a web of wrinkles. I tell her I'll make mac and cheese for dinner later and she tells us to sit down. "Your Pop-Pop isn't probably coming back," she tells us.

I don't know what I hear, but that's what she sounded like she said. I say, "What?"

"Your Pop-Pop," she says, and she shakes when she breathes, "isn't proba-bly coming back."

Blue sobs next to me.

minnows 2.1 My brother and me cross the empty field that's growing where it looks like a house should be there but it isn't, past the house that's haunted and its broke-out windows, and grab super-sour gooseberries from the gooseberry bush on our dirt path. The dirt path goes back into the woods here, and down at the end of it is the sewer grate and the big concrete pipe that pours into it. It's warm enough I'm sure I'm getting more pets today. The minnows will be swimming around in the sewer-pond, where concrete spills onto rocks and mud. Minnows maybe. Frogs even, maybe.

The woods are thicker here than back in the neighborhood, by the houses. But the pond is our secret. We can be pirates here, or Indians. We like pirates more, so we named it Pirate's Cove. I catch tadpoles and put pond water in my jar for them, then close the lid tight.

meal at the table, her anger hangs in the air, thick with sweat. And at 5:20, the whole house has got hotter, like it's gonna blow apart. And at 5:45, when Pop-Pop pulls up in the old white car, she's just waiting. She served the rest of us at 5:30, but she's just waiting.

In the tank, the goldfish chase and the water is getting hazy. Pop-Pop is a smog of Pabst Blue Ribbon and cigarettes and our mother's patience with him ran out long before he got his last ones for the road.

"Dinner at 5:30 means dinner at 5:30 in this house!" she shrieks. My ears ring. Blue starts to put his fingers in his ears, but I shake my head and make an *I'm serious* face and he stops.

And Pop-Pop is pleading with her, telling her he's sorry, he had car trouble, and she says bullshit, I smell the bar on you, and I have to admit she's right, already I noticed that, but I'm not no way gonna say it. And it explodes. They explode. They yell and she throws hot food and a skillet at him and Blue and I know we can't be around in the middle of one of these and we run for it.

1.1c In the night, I dream of Pop-Pop attacking the house, smashing in all of the ground-floor windows and yelling our mother's name. Gwen-Doe-Lyne is Our Mother's friend. She's still around, and that seems to make him angrier, 'cause she's an outsider. She don't understand.

Our mother tries to leave us. She's's stuck as we are. I wake to Gwen-Doe-Lyne and my mother smoking in the kitchen. "Careful there junior," she says, "Lotta glass broke here last night."

5.2 ~~Later,~~ I make our last box of mac and cheese and some powdered milk. ~~There's still a little powdered milk left after. July is burning out from under us and o~~ Our Pop-Pop is gone and I can't make our mother listen. I leave a bowl of mac and cheese outside her door, but know that in the morning it will be un-ate.

In the morning, the bowl of mac and cheese is right where I left it. Our mother hasn't touched it and she still isn't getting out of bed, **and our Pop-Pop still isn't around.**

4.2 In the morning I wake up to someone knocking on the front door. Outside is mMy Uncle Jim. He smiles and says "Mornin'. Your Pop-Pop here?"

"No," I tell him. "My mother says he might not come back."

Uncle Jim looks afraid, real afraid for a second, then wipes it off his face. "Where's she?" I point into the house.

Inside, the dishes have piled high and crusty and stuff is all over the carpets and floors.

"My God," says Uncle Jim. "Have you been eating?"

"Yeah!" I say. "I'm the man of the house now. I've been cooking."

Jim looks around at the dishes and the mess. "You're the man?"

"Yeah," I say, "Pop-Pop told me so before he left. It's family business, no one else's. We don't have to tell anyone. Especially not those pigs."

"Where's your phone?"

"We don't have to tell anyone," I say.

"Show me."

1.2 In the night, I dream of Pop-Pop attacking the house, smashing in all of the ground-floor windows and yelling our mother's name. Gwen-Doe-Lyne is Our Mother's friend. ~~She's still around,~~ and that seems to make him angrier, ~~'cause she's an outsider. She don't understand.~~

Our mother tries to leave us. ~~Our mother, though, will not leave us, not while that lid is held down tight.~~ She's's stuck as we are. ~~I wake to~~ Gwen-Doe-Lyne ~~and my mother smoking in the kitchen. "Careful there junior,"~~ she says, "Lotta glass broke here last night."

"Where's Pop-Pop?" I say.

"Where he belongs," says Gwen-Doe-Lyne. Our mother's eyes are unfocussed, reflecting.

0.8 Our mother is awake, but her eyes are dark all around and the skin there wrinkles dry in a web of wrinkles. "Your Pop-Pop isn't probably coming back," she tells us.

~~I don't know what I hear, but that's what she sounded like she said.~~ I say, "What?"

"Your Pop-Pop," she says, and she shakes when she breathes, "isn't probably coming back."

Blue sobs next to me, **and then the words are just shooting out of me. "Let him come back," I say.**

minnows 2.2 When our mother sees us, her eyes are puffy even though it's lunch time. The hit one isn't much more puffy than the not-hit one. But sitting there, in the kitchen, in rollers and a cloud of smoke from her smokes, she looks tired. Then her eyes find us through the clouds, and they get wide.

I hold up my jar and holler, "Tadpoles!" The tadpoles make me so happy I know they'll have to make her happy too. In the tank, one fish runs, the other chases.

Our mother pinches the cigarette between two fingers and points to the back porch. "Not in my house," she says, shaking her big, roller-lumpy head. "I keep a good home." She grinds out the butt, that's what my Pop-Pop calls it, her butt, in the too-full ashtray. She sneezes and ash swirls in the air, real slow, the sun through it like a giant sword.

I turn for the porch, but the jar slips and smashes on the floor, dumping sewer-pond water and breaking glass and flapping tadpoles in a big, slow crash.

3.2 In the morning I wake up to someone knocking on the front door. Outside, Gwen-Doe-Lyne and a cop car have pulled up.

Our mother is **silent and** shaking. **She has long scratches on her hands and her feet and her arms and her legs with black string like bugs' legs sticking out down both sides. Stitches. I've had stitches.**

~~"What'd you do to our mother?" I say.~~

~~She says, "I didn't do nothing. Your pop happened to her."~~

The cop is actually helping her up the front steps.

0.8a "I want him back. I want things back the way they were."

2.3 We're family, and families solve their own problems. **None of the other kids talk about their pops hitting their moms—that's not how we do it.** We police our own, no cops, Pop-Pop said to us. Even Uncle Jim beats up Pop-Pop in private. It's no one else's business.

4.3 My Uncle Jim smiles and says

"Have you been eating?"
"I'm the man of the house now. I've been cooking."
"You're the man?"
"Yeah," I say, "Pop-Pop told me so before he left. It's family business, no one else's. We don't have to tell anyone. Especially not those pigs." **Uncle Jim jumps a bit at my words. He knocks on our mother's door, says her name. Then he comes back to me.**
"Where's your phone?"
"We don't have to tell anyone," I say.
"Show me."
I lead him into the kitchen and show him the phone on the wall. He picks it up, then gives it a funny look and hits the button a few times. Then he puts it back, shaking his head.
"Do you have any friends who live close?" he says.

0.7 Our mother is awake, but her eyes are dark all around and the skin there wrinkles dry in a web of wrinkles. "Your Pop-Pop isn't probably coming back," she tells us.
I say, "What?"
"Your Pop-Pop," she says, and she shakes when she breathes, "isn't probably coming back."
~~Blue sobs next to me, and then t~~ The words are just shooting out of me. "Let him come back," I say. **She says, "I don't want to."**

minnows 2.3 ~~When o~~ Our mother sees us, ~~her eyes are puffy even though it's lunch time. The hit one isn't much more puffy than the not-hit one. But sitting there, in the kitchen, in rollers and a cloud of smoke from her smokes, she looks tired. Then her eyes find us through the clouds, and they get wide.~~

"How the hell did you boys get so filthy? It's not even lunchtime!" she says. I look down at my shirt and see the dirt and mud. Blue is worse, though, he's got mud in his ears somehow.

I turn for the porch, but the jar slips and smashes on the floor, dumping sewer-pond water and breaking glass and flapping tadpoles in a big, slow crash. Our mother hits the roof, screaming at us to look at the mess we made and clean up the mess we made. Blue bolts out the front door and I scramble out the screen window with no screen in it, onto the thing that's supposed to hold up an air conditioner, and away. I sneak a big canning jar from Pop-Pop's rusty lawnmower shed. I catch more tadpoles at Pirate's Cove and chase minnows. Blue finds me there after a while, tells me he wants to go home. "Not yet," I say. "Let her cool off. You see how she goes after Pop-Pop. We'll go later."

0.7a "~~I want him back.~~ I want things back the way they were!"

".were they way the back things want I"

0.6 ~~Our mother is awake, but her eyes are dark all around and the skin there wrinkles dry in a web of wrinkles. "Your Pop-Pop isn't probably coming back," she tells us.~~

~~I say, "What?"~~

~~"Your Pop-Pop," she says, and she shakes when she breathes, "isn't probably coming back."~~

The words are just shooting out of me. "Let him come back," I say. She says, "I don't want to."

This is insane. We're a family.

I make each word weigh the same. "Let. Him. Come. Back."

"I don't want to," she says, and her voice is sad, so sad.

"Why are you so sad? All you have to do is let him come back," I say.

Later, I make our last box of mac and cheese and some powdered milk. There's still a little powdered milk left after. July is burning out from under us and our Pop-Pop is gone and I can't make our mother listen. I leave a bowl of mac and cheese outside her door, but know that in the morning it will be un-ate.

1.3 ~~In the night, I dream of Pop-Pop attacking the house, smashing in all of the ground-floor windows and yelling our mother's name. Gwen-Doe-Lyne is Our Mother's friend. She's still around, and that seems to make him angrier, 'cause she's an outsider. She don't understand.~~ *The four of us are on a beach at Lake Okoboji. We're swimming in Lake Okoboji, water that's clear like glass. The rocks on the bottom are exactly the shape and size of turtles, and I can barely pick one up to swim with it to the top to prove to everyone it's a turtle, and when I get there, it has turned into a rock to fool me. I try and try, but the turtles keep turning into rocks until finally my Pop-Pop, shaking his head, tells me to knock it off.*

Then we're all four, our mother, Blue, me, and my Pop-Pop in the lead, swimming, but the water is dirtier than Okoboji, because it's Pirate's Cove, and we're minnows, and gigantic people appear right over the top of us and try to catch us. Pop-Pop and our mother chase all wild, one thumping into the other, both hurting both, till one, Pop-Pop leaves through the roof of the pond and swims up, out, and away. In the commotion the water has gotten swirled up and hard to see through, but a big blade of sun cuts down through the swirl. My lungs burn and a net scrapes across my face and body and sploosh, I'm in a fish tank. With a thunk, a rock the size and shape of a turtle lands on the lid—a rock bigger than any of us.

Our mother tries to leave us. Our mother, though, will not leave us, not while that lid is held down tight. She's's stuck as we are. ~~Gwen-Doe-Lyne says, "Lotta glass broke here last night."~~

~~"Where's Pop-Pop?" I say.~~

~~"Where he belongs," says Gwen-Doe-Lyne.~~ Our mother's eyes are unfocused, reflecting. Like a fish's.

o.6a "I want things back the way they were!"

"I want things back the way they were!"

o.5 The words are just shooting out of me. "Let him come back," I say. She says, "I don't want to."

This is insane. We're a family.

I make each word weigh the same. "Let. Him. Come. Back."

"I don't want to," she says, and her voice is sad, so sad.

"Why are you so sad? All you have to do is let him come back," I say.

"It isn't that easy," she says. I look around, and I want it all to make sense and it doesn't. The fish tank is thick with algae and swirled-up stuff. Our Mother drifts, her eyes dull like a deep-sea fish's, one that doesn't use its eyes much. It still doesn't make sense.

Interstitial 1.2 In the woods along our path, Boy-O Sparks and the other older boys swing and jump through the trees, hooting like chimps. When he's around the older boys, Boy-O doesn't want much to do with us. We know to stay out later still when we see the red lights flashing from our place.

We catch lightning bugs and smear their glowing stuff on our faces for war paint, until the lightning bugs aren't out anymore and the glowing stuff doesn't glow anymore. We get back late to no one at home. Broken dishes and food exploded all over. I dig around in the kitchen and find us peanut butter and jelly and make us one-slice Wonder Bread sandwiches and wild berry Kool-Aid. Blue seems real, real sad, but he gets a red Kool-Aid mustache, and when I show him in the mirror, he laughs. The phone rings but I don't pick it up. No one told me what we're supposed to tell anyone who asks. And like Pop-Pop said, we're a family. We fix our own problems. They're no one else's business.

Blue and I got lots of bug bites outside tonight. I find the pink lotion our mother uses for those and paint them all pink.

"I'll make us mac and cheese," I say. In my head I can hear Pop-Pop, my Pop-Pop, telling Blue to listen to me, telling me to take care of Our Mother, telling me I'm the man of the house. "It'll be okay. I'm the man of the house." *Don't take too much shit from'er, but take care of'er*, he'd said.

minnows 2.4 We don't dare go back for lunch. I let Blue drop the minnows he catches in my jar with my tadpoles. The tadpoles won't mind. It keeps him too busy to worry about going back yet.

When we get back, we go in through the back door and I put this jar on a shelf on the back porch, real, real careful. Blue says to me something about fish needing air, and that's stupid, fish breathe water, so I tell him to shut up.

Our mother is in bed again, and Pop-Pop is still. In the kitchen I find Wonder Bread and steak sauce and make us no-steak steak sandwiches. I mix an envelope of Kool-Aid in a plastic pitcher in the sink and stir with my hand in almost to the elbow to reach the bottom. The goldfish are still alive in that tank. One of the goldfish hits the lid so hard it flips a little open, then claps back closed.

minnows 3.1 When our mother wakes for the afternoon she takes a long, long time showering. There's sticky red on the counter where I spilled pouring us Kool-Aid, and ashy mud near the ashtray. Our mother steps from her room, calls us gross little monsters, and orders us to the back yard. She hoses the mud off of us and says our clothes are done for.

In the night, I hear the goldfish chasing, chasing, and once in a while, the thump of the one or the other one hitting the lid.

0.5a "I want things back the way they were!"

"I want things back the way they were!"

0.4 ~~Our mother is awake, but her eyes are dark all around and the skin there wrinkles dry in a web of wrinkles. "Your Pop-Pop isn't probably coming back," she tells us.~~

~~I say, "What?"~~

~~"Your Pop-Pop," she says, and she shakes when she breathes, "isn't probably coming back."~~

The words are just shooting out of me. "Let him come back," I say.

She says, "I don't want to."

This is insane. We're a family.

I make each word weigh the same. "Let. Him. Come. Back."

"I don't want to," she says, and her voice is sad, so sad.

"Why are you so sad? All you have to do is let him come back," I say.

Later, I make our last box of mac and cheese and some powdered milk. There's still a little powdered milk left after. July is burning out from under us and our Pop-Pop is gone and I can't make our mother listen. I leave a bowl of mac and cheese outside her door, but know that in the morning it will be un-ate.

Everything zeroes here.

minnows 3.2 In the morning, on the back porch, the tadpoles and the minnows float at the top of the closed-lidded jar. In the dining room the goldfish pester each other.

0.4a I make each word weigh the same. "Let. Him. Come. Back."

"I don't want to," she says, ~~and her voice is sad, so sad.~~

~~"Why are you so sad? All you have to do is let him come back," I say.~~

~~"It isn't that easy," she says. I look around, and I want it all to make sense and it doesn't.~~ The fish tank is thick with algae and swirled-up stuff. Our Mother drifts, her eyes dull like a deep-sea fish's, one that doesn't use its eyes much. ~~It still doesn't make sense.~~

Everything zeroes here. In four . . .

fishie 1.2 *What's fish food taste like?!* This I had not thought of asking. "It smells like Pirate's Cove mud," I say.

"Yeah, but what does it *taste* like?"

"It's good. Like catfish. Here, stick out your tongue."

Blue smiles and out comes his tongue. I smear it with a really, really big pinch, and Blue's smile disappears in a burst of barf that covers his chin, but doesn't go anywhere else. It won't be good if our mother sees it. I drag him into my brother's and me's bathroom and washcloth him off.

0.3 Our Mother drifts, her eyes dull like a deep-sea fish's, one that doesn't use its eyes much. It still doesn't make sense.

"I'll make us mac and cheese," I say. In my head I can hear Pop-Pop, my Pop-Pop, telling Blue to listen to me, telling me to take care of our mother, telling me I'm the man of the house. ~~"It'll be okay. I'm the man of the house."~~ *Don't take too much shit from 'er,* ~~but take care of 'er,~~ he'd said.

Our mother says my name, Pop-Pop's name, and I explode, looking for weakness.

~~Everything zeroes here. In four~~ **three** . . .

4.4 "We don't have to tell anyone," I say.

I lead him into the kitchen and show him the phone on the wall. He picks it up, then gives it a funny look and hits the button a few times. Then he puts it back, shaking his head.

"Do you have any friends who live close?" he says.

I nod. "Boy-O and his family the Sparkses are only a mile and a half or so down."

Uncle Jim thumbs through the phone book and writes out a number on our notepad and hands it to me. "I need you to go to Boy-O's house and tell his pop you have an emergency, and to get an ambulance here."

0.2 Our Mother drifts, her eyes dull like a deep-sea fish's.

"I'll make us mac and cheese," I say. In my head I can hear Pop-Pop, my Pop-Pop, telling Blue to listen to me, telling me to take care of our mother, telling me I'm the man of the house. *Don't take too much shit from'er* he'd said.

Our mother says my name, Pop-Pop's name, and I explode, looking for weakness.

~~three~~ **two** . . .

0.1 ~~Our mother says my name, Pop-Pop's name, and~~ I'm ~~explode,~~ looking for weakness **in her**. I point to her cuts from the flying glass.

"You let him come back or I'll hit you in the stitches!"

Our mother's mouth opens big and round for a second, then closes, and her eyes glaze over, dead like a carp's. Her mouth opens again, big and round, but I can't hear any air going in or out. She stands, wobbly, and drifts into her room, closing the door. Then we hear the click of the lock locking.

~~two~~ **one** . . .

minnows 3.3 In the dining room the goldfish pester each other. **They're going crazy in that tank.**

0.0 I point to ~~her~~ **Our Mother's** cuts from the flying glass.

"You let him come back or I'll hit you in the stitches!"

Our mother's mouth opens big and round for a second, then closes, and her eyes glaze over, dead like a carp's. Her mouth opens again, big and round, but I can't hear any air going in or out. She stands, wobbly, and drifts into her room, closing the door. Then we hear the click of the lock locking.

3.3 ~~In the morning I wake up to someone knocking on the front door. Outside, Gwen-Doe-Lyne and a cop car have pulled up.~~

~~The cop is actually helping her up the front steps.~~

"You the man of the house?" says the cop. He seems friendly. That's not right. I nod, wary.

"Your pop gave her quite a scare tonight," says the cop.

I nod. *We police our own,* I think.

"Know where he's keeping himself?" says the cop. I knew it. He wants us to break ranks, rat each other out. "Nope," I say, then realize it's true. Pop-Pop was never happy to see the cops visit. Why should I be any different?

4.5 ~~"We don't have to tell anyone," I say.~~

~~I lead him into the kitchen and show him the phone on the wall. He picks it up, then gives it a funny look and hits the button a few times. Then he puts it back, shaking his head.~~

~~"Do you have any friends who live close?" he says.~~

~~I nod. "Boy-O and his family the Sparkses are only a mile and a half or so down."~~

Uncle Jim thumbs through the phone book and writes out a number on our notepad and hands it to me. "I need you to go to Boy-O's house and tell his pop you have an emergency, and to get an ambulance here."

"Aye-aye, cap'n," I say. It's a game: I'll be a pirate on a secret mission from my pirate captain.

He watches me for a second, then returns my salute.

"Go *now*," he says.

THE STORK

Sharif Shakhshir

A wingful of lies
pointed towards the nursery,
It seems you were delivered
the wrong model.
The XGP-22s get caught in community college,
end up working an office job,
have hip dysplasia in old age, and
enjoy sex with other women
when alcohol is involved,
but with the right pills
can be happy.
They looked at you,
your parents, the way a couple with a small apartment
looks at a puppy's large paws.

You were supposed to get an XLJ-1:
a boy
who loves vegetables,
studies medicine,
enjoys taking care of the elderly,
and has a heart
equipped with extra room for Jesus.
Mother and Father rehearsed what
they would tell their friends:
how you weren't theirs to love and
how it was the right thing to do,

then they placed you
in my finger feathers.
I'll be back
with your corrected order
shortly, I assured them.
Father handed you your teddy.
You grabbed it with your slender fingers—his,
and said goodbye with your brown eyes—hers.
They thanked me for my trouble.
Closed the door.
Probably wondering if they should have
bothered to get my business card or
a tracking code for their new son.

Don't cry, baby XGP-22. You have your teddy bear and
the song of six little hungry storks
to calm you as the water comes to a boil.

IT HAPPENED TO PAUL SESCAU

Patrick Cole

Looking in the mirror in the employee restroom of the bookstore, Paul Sescau reviewed the events of the preceding days, searching for clues to what was happening to him. In retrospect, he could see signs that something had been afoot. But at the time, the events didn't add up to anything other than the usual accumulated mix of cheery uncertainty, malaise, and slight strangeness that characterized his normal life. And he couldn't see how the events of his recent days added up to a formula for what he had only a moment before discovered was overtaking him. Perhaps there was no recipe for it. It was different every time, or it was a kind of alchemy, a paradoxical science, certain in its rules, though those rules could not be understood or even discovered with purely rational, scientific methods.

When he left work on the previous Thursday, Paul enjoyed, as always, his walk up St. John's Boulevard, reviewing the benches crowded with old men and women talking about the things only they knew, and the children in the playgrounds there, and the late afternoon sky with its clouds peering over the edge of apartment buildings at all the activity, some lingering over side streets looking for a better view.

Then the feeling he had forgotten something at the office swept over him. He mentally reviewed all the papers that were relevant to him at that time, and all the projects he had worked on or discussed that day, and couldn't think of anything he needed to take home with him. Still the feeling persisted. He shrugged it off and kept walking, but a block later, it returned to him even more powerfully. What the hell, he thought. He stopped and stood still and thought, like a statue of a Concentrating Man, the other pedestrians walking around, flashing their eyes at him.

When Paul had the feeling that he was missing something, or that he had forgotten something, the feeling was almost certainly true. A pause, a thought, and he could recall the missing thing. But this time, no amount of concentration helped him explain the feeling. A useful instinct had suddenly rebelled. Or the feeling had accidentally shot out of his brain circuitry. Now it appeared to serve no purpose, though it was confident, eager.

And this feeling was to return again and again in the following days, always a cipher, leading him to wonder where his brain's private evolution was leading him.

Paul then learned that he was two years older than he had thought. He and his wife had friends over for a potluck dinner, with the guests bringing mystery plates and surprise bottles of wine and booze. After eating, one of their friends asked how old Paul was, and he automatically said "37."

His wife started laughing, as if he'd made a joke.

"What?" he said to her suspiciously.

And she said, "If you're going to lie about it, Paul, you should take a little more off. Go for 30 or 32."

"I'm 37," he said sincerely. Everyone laughed. He looked at them.

"Paul is 39," Valerie told them.

"I'm 37," he insisted, with a smile.

"Almost 40," Valerie said.

What the hell? How old am I? He tried to think about it. He asked himself the question again to see what immediate answer came to mind. But nothing came to mind. Just a blank. He didn't know.

Then he tried to figure it out. Fine, he said to himself. What year was I born? But nothing definitive came up then, either. He tried harder, and a year arose in his mind but it slid quickly away, and all the other years around it, before and after, sounded equally true. None of them in particular cried out for attention, none identified themselves with him, none seemed to have anything to say about Paul Sescau—though he remembered feeling before, during his entire lifetime, that the year of his birth and he were tightly intertwined.

What else, Paul thought, as he looked at his reflection in the mirror. Some greater context.

There was the dilemma. The philosophical problem that Paul had been aware of over the course of his life but which had only recently kicked in, suddenly becoming acute, worrying. It was the simple problem of life on this earth: it seemed like one big anxiety attack. There was working life, the concern about being treated fairly, making enough money, having enough for future goals such as raising a family and retirement. There was personal life, and the worry about not reading enough good books, not enjoying peaceful moments enough, not knowing how to live in the present moment. And the end of the equation: if the working life and personal life were in order, time still passed, and all the gains were wiped away by death. All the striving was to no purpose. Stress was inevitable but useless.

Something ticked over in his mind, perhaps something programmed to do just that at a certain point, or something triggered by other age-related changes, and he found himself preoccupied not with death, but with life—what to do with it. What was the project here? What were we trying to accomplish? He felt as though there had been a meeting about this a long time ago explaining everything, but he had missed it. Why do we live?

Paul had a good job. He had some savings. He had a wonderful wife. They were talking about having a child. They could afford it. They were taking a wine-tasting course, planning their vacation. By earth's standards, they had it made. They had time to think about the news, time to read a little. Time to wonder. But now wondering was an urgent matter.

Paul discussed the dilemma with Valerie. He was actually somewhat embarrassed to admit it was getting him down, that something he considered a cliché could affect him so. "Where does it come from?" he asked her.

"It's just that thing inside," she said. "It's inside us all, we just don't notice it. And it ripens and matures over time. And sometimes it comes to the surface."

"Good God," Paul said.

"You don't have to worry, Paul. It's in all of us and it affects all of us to some extent."

"But it doesn't seem to bother anybody else so much. Everyone else just seems to live with it."

"I don't know," she said in a high, skeptical voice. "You'd be surprised how many people are disturbed by it."

"But what am I supposed to do? Every time something good happens, I feel great. But then I think, So what?"

She tilted her head to the side. "Sweetheart, don't worry. In the vast majority of cases, it just settles down."

"It doesn't go away, though."

"Well, no, I think in most people it never goes away. This is something we are all born with and it lives with us forever, in symbiosis. It may disturb some people, but most get used to it."

Paul shook his head. "How could they ever do that?"

Coming back to the surface, to the days leading up to his reviewing himself in the restroom mirror, we see that Paul started getting what appeared to be a cold. A tickle developed deep within his nose, which he didn't even notice at first, but then his nose became stuffed up. That was the only symptom. He kept sniffling and sniffling but the blockage would not abate.

What else.

A gaggle of Buddhist monks arrived in town, flowing about from place to place in their red ochre robes. Everyone saw them, drifting together into and out of the subway stations, flowing across zebra crossings, flowing down the broad avenues towards the sea. No one seemed to know exactly where they came from or what they were doing there so suddenly, but unlike other random events and curiosities which continually distract the city, it was comforting to Paul that they were there, as if a new plant had somehow learned how to bloom in this hard place.

From the first moment he caught sight of them, standing together in a sandy area in the park, Paul wanted to speak with them, to ask them what they were doing in town, naturally, but more to ask them what they knew, how could they help. But though they always seemed to be in good spirits, wearing calm smiles, Paul was intimidated. He didn't want to be rude and interrupt whatever it was they were doing, whatever it was they were living. He knew that he also did not want to be confronted by his own ignorance. It seemed easier, though it was endlessly frustrating, to ignore them, this potential source of wisdom, this certain source of mystery.

Over dinner, Paul's wife asked if he had a cold. He said No and then he said Yes. He thought about it and realized he had been vaguely aware of his sniffling and that it had been going on for some time. Yet he didn't feel bad. And his nose didn't run. It just seemed stuffed. Valerie advised him to take something for it.

Paul noticed that his dilemma was hard to separate from simple sadness. What differentiated it, though, was that it was brought on by normal life, or even by joy, instead of being provoked by something sad in itself. Something normal or something nice was put in a different light, in greater context, and it became sad. Paul found he could miss something, long for it, even in the moment he was experiencing it. It was melancholy.

Paul lay on the sofa one afternoon reading. It was a long, well-written, award-winning book on the Boer War. He was enjoying it tremendously; the Boer War was like a kind of candy, and it tasted better the more one ate. Now and then, he would shift position on the couch and realize there were only so many ways to hold such a heavy book and be comfortable. Then he would look at the book, calculate how much he had read, how long it had taken him, and at what rate in pages per hour he was reading. The book was a large investment in time. Some pages, outliers, took four or five minutes to get through. His brain looked at it this way: Avg. 2 min/pg x 650 = 1300; 1300/60 = 21 hrs, 1 hr/day = 21 days, approx. 1 month. One month, if he took no days off. How many such books would he have time to read in his life? What would his knowledge of the Boer War do for him? Was he somehow being fooled by its sugary taste?

Was this the best book for him to be reading, the most important for him, Paul Sescau? How could one find that most important book?—surely he had passed right by it in the bookstore, and never even known it.

He got up and went to the window, opened it and leaned out. And looking to the left, he saw his wife. She was returning from her outing on her bicycle, a baguette in the front basket. He smiled and called out to her as she approached; she looked up and waved and rang her bicycle bell.

The sound of the bell was like a signal. Wonderful, it said. And Paul heard it, and thought about it. How wonderful this is—my beautiful wife, coming home, on her bicycle, on a sunny day, with fresh bread. He loved her, he loved the moment. How lucky I am to have these moments, thought Paul.

But then he turned away from the window. And the sweet feeling intensified. It was as if the heart was like the tongue, with the sides sensitive to sourness, the back sensitive to bitterness, the front sensing sweetness. He could feel his heart curling up in response to the sweetness, salivating.

Then his brain kicked in. How good life can be. But it isn't always so, and after it is good for a moment, it changes. And there will be a time when I no longer receive moments like the one I just had. And when my wife doesn't. Not when we are old, or when one or both of us is dead. It will be tomorrow, in a year, or another inevitable year. The moment won't be the same because it won't be now, with us in this place, this apartment, her with that bicycle, us at our present ages. This lifetime. It won't be now: when we lived at number 260 on Offenbach, when I wasn't yet the boss, we hadn't yet had kids, she still rode her bike everywhere. We might get other types of moments for other ages, other life stages, other places. But today's moments will be gone.

And then the other moments will be gone.

Paul met one of the monks. On his days off, he liked to walk around town taking pictures. He was sitting on a bench fiddling with the camera, when someone said to him: "Are you a photographer?"

He looked up, sniffled, and saw that it was one of the red-robed monks, smiling pleasantly. Paul told him he wasn't a photographer, just someone who liked to take pictures. "You look like a photographer," the monk said. It was a compliment of some kind, Paul thought. The monk sat down and said he was also someone who liked to take pictures and then he joked that he himself did not look like a photographer. The monk noted that Paul had an old camera, and Paul said that it was simple but it had everything you needed and it was a solid chunk of metal.

"It will surely outlive me," he said.

"Like your photographs," the monk said. Then he told Paul how he had gone to a photography shop in town and they had some antique cameras. They also had a couple of old photo albums, from the 1930s and 40s, oblong books with thick, solid covers into which the owners had pasted black and white pictures. The shop owner said the people who had made them were long dead. He said he was at a loss for what to do with them. The monk bought them.

"It's curious, isn't it?" the monk asked Paul.

Paul agreed without at first realizing that the monk had starting talking about the dilemma which had come to dominate Paul's psyche. Then he realized it, and wondered how it was possible that it had taken a moment to do so. He cursed himself for his short metaphysical attention span. Then he sniffled and said that lately he had given a lot of thought to exactly this kind of thing. And he sniffled again. "It seems strange," he said, "that people accumulate experiences and souvenirs and pictures of people dear to them and of the highest points in their lives, and then they die. And eventually the pictures and souvenirs get taken out to the street because they belong to no one anymore." Then he sniffled more and the monk asked if he had a cold, and Paul assumed that he had changed the subject.

"I guess so," he said. "My nose is stuffed up." He sniffled for emphasis. "I tried taking something but it just got worse. I tried something else but now my nose is more blocked than ever."

"I see," the monk said.

"I'm going to try something else, and if that doesn't work, I'll try something else again, I suppose," Paul said, sniffling above his smile.

"I see," the monk said. Then there was long pause in which Paul looked around him. And then the monk said, "Once you start a war, it is very difficult to stop."

Paul remembered this, in the restroom of the bookstore, thinking, If that's not a clue, I don't know what is. His memories were now catching up to him in the present moment.

This day was a Saturday, and that morning Valerie had slept in. The sun was shining and he had a number of errands he was looking forward to running. Paul loved errands, little bite-sized problems that could be dispatched quickly and completely, items checked off of lists. It felt like progress, and Paul was addicted to progress. His only distraction that morning was his clogged nose, and he realized then that only his left nostril was affected. The feeling in the nostril evoked an image of an overly thick cork stuck in the thin neck of a green bottle. The various medications he had tried were of no avail, and neither were violent attempts at nose-blowing while pinching his clear right nostril.

He began the day looking for new shoes. He found a large store and walked around looking at the left-foot shoes displayed on miniature shelves on the wall. He was relieved when none of the salespeople bothered him and he could browse in peace. But when he found a model he wanted to try, he couldn't get anyone's attention. He tried waving, and calling out with a blunt Eh! but no one came to him, and it even seemed that one or two of the salespeople saw him and ducked into the stockroom. Typical, he thought.

He got annoyed, and this was exacerbated by his constant impulse to sniffle and its constant failure, a total lack of movement of air through his left nostril. And when he spoke, he heard a faint echo of his own voice in his head. He finally managed to flag down a saleswoman who seemed rather uncertain of herself. She avoided making eye contact and hastily disappeared into the back as soon as he said what he wanted. She brought him the shoes and they were not the size he'd requested, but when he tried to stop the saleswoman again, she went blazing past him to help other customers. Exasperated, he gave up and hit the street.

What he didn't know was that something thick and black was peeking out from his left nostril.

He next went into a music store nearby to ask about tickets for a concert Valerie was interested in, a woman who sang Edith Piaf songs. There was a skinny young man behind the counter busy staring at a computer screen. "Yeah," the young man said without looking up. Paul asked about the Edith Piaf concert.

The clerk looked up at Paul and his stare stuck to Paul's face for a long moment. Then he shook his head and looked back at the computer screen.

"No, really," Paul said. "Not *the* Edith Piaf, someone who sings like Edith Piaf. Edith Piaf is dead, I know that."

"Dude," the clerk said without looking up, as if that was a statement in itself. And then nothing.

"Can you help me or what?" Paul said. The clerk looked at Paul again, shaking his head: "We on one of those hidden camera shows or something?"

"Look, I just want a couple of tickets to the Edith Piaf thing. You got them or not?"

And then the clerk's look suddenly changed. He seemed a little frightened as he swung his face back to his computer and stared blankly at it.

"Edith Piaf," Paul said.

"Yeah, okay, okay, I'm working on it," the clerk said, and started punching up the order. What a day I'm having, Paul thought. He didn't know that a slick worm was now hanging out of his left nostril. It was jet black and sparkled like coal and was so thick that it deformed the shape of his nose. He didn't feel a thing.

For lunch Paul went to a deli several blocks away, where he ordered a sandwich and a beer at the counter, on guard for further lapses in service. He suddenly got the feeling that he was forgetting something, something very important, but he was getting used to that now.

At the counter the deli guys were brusque and curt, but they always were, and Paul was relieved to be taken care of rapidly. The place was crowded and the only table available was a small round one in the middle of the room. There was no chair next to it but there was an unoccupied one at a table nearby. Paul approached that table and placed his hand on the back of the empty chair and asked if he could use it. The couple at the table nodded vigorously and Paul slid the chair away to the empty table and plopped down heavily. He ate his sandwich distractedly, concentrating on how to be alone in a crowded room. The nose-snake had dropped still further out of his nose, falling as far as his upper lip.

There was a bookstore near the deli that Paul liked, but he debated stopping in because it wasn't on his list; he had a stack of books waiting to be read on his bedroom shelf. But Paul loved books. He loved to read, always wished he had more time for it, and books were his favorite things to buy. It was something about their shape, how convenient they were to cradle and carry in the hand, their slick covers. Something about them told Paul, "Have." They were presents, each and every one of them, like knowledge in solid form, almost edible.

So he entered the bookshop and waved and smiled at the guy behind the counter who he recognized and who recognized him, though they didn't know each other's names. First he wandered around the Fiction section, perusing the shelves. All the old names there, as always, Bellow, Dreiser, Faulkner, Hemingway . . . Joyce, Kafka, Orwell, Updike, Roth. All dead, their books still here. Surely they didn't give a shit anymore. Hell, Hemingway stopped giving a shit when he was still alive. And then there were the thousands of lesser-known authors surrounding them.

Well, Paul thought. Roth's not dead. But he will be.

He walked past the History section then Art/Architecture then Social Sciences and then entered a dark wood paneled room containing Wisdom. Wisdom was housed in two sets of shelves running from floor to ceiling, each about five feet wide. He stood back and looked at the entire section.

Wisdom. There it was. What could be the problem?

And then a thing happened which struck him as odd. A woman

wandered into the room and past him and started examining the books. He stepped forward and joined her. At one point, she wanted to get to the other side of him and said Excuse me. He looked at her and smiled warmly and she went around. He went back to concentrating on the titles. One of the books had a Buddhist monk on the cover, a monk dressed just like the one he had recently met, with a red robe, but sitting in the lotus position. Paul looked at the monk and then turned to look at the woman, who was standing stock-still next to him. He felt a tickle in his nose and sniffled loudly but his nostril was absolutely and utterly blocked. He shook his head curtly from side to side. Then the woman clutched her stomach, doubled over, gagged, and stumbled towards the front of the store. Others at the front tried to attend to her but she continued out onto the street.

The book in Paul's hand was a classic called *Killing the Buddha*. He turned back to it, his eyes wide. Eventually he decided to forget about the woman and started leafing through the book. Then he brought it to the counter. And that's when he found out what was going on.

He put the book down on the counter and took out his wallet, mentally preparing small talk about the strange woman who had just run out. But his anonymous friend at the register looked at him and said, "Are you all right?" There was a great deal of concern in his voice and in his sad, book-reading eyes.

"Yes," Paul said. "Why?"

"You don't look so good." He pronounced *you* in a skeptical, elongated way, like Yoooooooooou don't look so good.

And Paul didn't look so good. He would agree with that assessment after entering the employee restroom and looking in the mirror. In fact, he nearly passed out. The woman beside him in the Wisdom section must have watched as the squirming black worm slid out a couple more inches.

Paul's review of his recent life did not allow him to escape it. He refused the offer of an ambulance and raced home from the bookstore on foot, his arm covering his face like the villain in a silent movie. He was relieved to find Valerie had gone out, because he did not know how to break the news to her. He stood in the bathroom and forced himself to look at himself in the mirror. He stared in amazement at the faceless black nose-snake, gently touching it, watching it wiggle slightly in response. Sometimes it wafted gently from side to side on its own. He tried lightly tugging on it, but it would not budge further. He washed his hands, avoiding his appearance in the mirror, then sat on the toilet, wondering why this was happening to him.

He heard her come in to the apartment and he shut the bathroom door. He would not come out and would not let her in when she knocked to see if he was all right. In telling her to go away Paul noticed how his voice had become absurdly pinched and nasal. "Leave me alone!" he whined pathetically when she insisted.

"What's going on in there?" Valerie demanded, baffled.

"You won't believe it. I'm warning you . . . It's horrible, disgusting. You won't . . . you won't be able to handle it."

"Jesus Christ, Paul! I'm your wife!"

He cracked open the door.

"I can handle anything," she continued. "It's my duty to handle anything. Women aren't pussies, like men. Christ." She peered inside. He was covering his face. "What . . . " she said, and he lowered his arm.

"It's coming out," he said, and her face fell and her knees wobbled, but she did not faint.

They planned their strategy. Paul called into work the following Monday to say that he would not be in. He told his boss he had a personal problem and couldn't say when it would be resolved. The boss didn't say anything at first. But then, as a way of trying to learn what Paul's personal problem was, he said, "Well, now, Paul, if there's anything we can help you with, you just let us know. I mean, I'm sure we can help out somehow with whatever problem it is you are having . . . "

"I've got a worm," Paul said, unwilling to play games. "A huge black worm coming out of my nose."

The boss was silent for a long moment. "Worm leave," he said at last, considering it. "What you're asking for is worm leave. Of course that's covered in the employee handbook. You certainly can take time for that. Worm leave is indefinite. So you just relax there, and, well, I wish you luck with that."

Paul thanked him.

"Let us know how it comes out," the boss said.

Paul and Valerie spent hours looking up information on the internet, which was generally contradictory, panic-inducing, and superstitious but occasionally—though only temporarily—soothing. It was the equivalent of someone standing up at a baseball game and shouting to the crowd, "Have any of you ever had a rash like this?" They got a doctor's appointment for Wednesday. Paul held a white handkerchief to his face the entire way to the doctor's office.

The doctor prescribed what they call watchful waiting. You wait and see what happens, paying close attention. "The worst-case scenario," the doctor explained, "is that the snake goes back inside."

"What do we do if that happens?" Valerie asked.

Looking at Paul, the doctor said, "In that case, you can resume normal life. But that part's beyond our control." Then he held up his hands to emphasize another point. "The key thing is, if it comes all the way out, you must take immediate action to make sure it does not go back in again. And it will try mightily to do so."

The waiting began. They measured the length of worm that extended from Paul's nose, so they could monitor its progress. But nothing seemed to happen. Days passed, with Paul unwilling to go outside. He read, he did home repair projects, he cooked. He grew terribly bored. He missed work. At first he continually asked his wife, the bathroom mirror, the walls, the street he viewed from the window: "Why is this happening to me?" When Valerie tried to reassure him, he said he hadn't wanted this thing. It was unfair. He wanted to be left alone, to live a normal life.

After three weeks, the black snake had slid down only another centimeter and a half. From what the doctor had told them, there could be much further to go. Now Paul grew resentful, not of his situation, but of society. "Goddamn nose-snake," he thought. "I just want to get a drink in a bar." Why should he be trapped inside by this? Why should he suffer? He hadn't asked for it. He was a human being, for crying out loud. "I will not be a pariah!" he told his wife. She nodded her head.

Paul and Valerie arrived first that evening and took seats at the large table surrounded by ten empty chairs. The worm was now hanging over his lips, but he acted as if he didn't notice. As the others in the class arrived, Paul sat up straight and held his chin high. They came in smiling, but when saying hello to Paul they fairly shuddered with surprise, sometimes barely able to choke out the remainder of their greeting. Paul replied by saying "Hello" and "How are you?" with deliberate clarity. The others bowed their heads as they took their seats, saying "Fine," without looking back at him.

When all ten seats were filled there was silence as those on the side of the table opposite Paul stared at the table top or pretended to be studying their notes. At last the professor arrived and, seeing Paul, he immediately turned away to write on the white board. He wrote Bordeaux, then hesitated, not wanting to turn back around. He wrote Burgundy. Then he wrote Alsace, Loire, Rhône . . . Languedoc-Roussillon, Provence. He paused. Then, Champagne. Pause. Bergerac. Before long he had written about every place name in France he could think of. He hesitated, and then drew a map.

When they each had their empty wine glasses in front of them, Paul stared at his as if it were a sculpture, with its feminine curves, the widened hips, the Venus of Willendorf. The professor went around the room pouring a bottle, as Paul thought about women evolving wide hips to facilitate the birth of large human babies, these wide hips giving women a particular sway when they walk, men finding this movement attractive, assisting mating . . . Funny who we are.

The professor returned to the front of the class. "Cabernet Sauvignon," he said. "Let's have a look at the color." The class rapidly raised their glasses and tilted them forward, concentrating gravely on the innocent wine's color, grateful to have something to look at. Paul pretended everything was normal. Valerie held his hand under the table.

Usually they discussed the color. But this time the professor simply said, "Let's give it a go" and took a sip. Most of the students acted as if they didn't know what to do, appearing nauseated. Paul enthusiastically brought his glass towards his mouth but it ran into the greasy black snake hanging in front of his lips, spilling some wine onto the table and onto the snake. The snake wiggled. He shifted the glass to his left hand, held the snake back with his right hand, and took a sip. He let go of the snake, held his head aloft with the wine in his mouth. He opened his mouth slightly, forming a small O. The others squirmed, almost unable to look away, as he drew air in, making a gurgling sound. Paul wore an expression of great concentration for several seconds, then closed his mouth, swallowed, and smiled broadly. The wine had a strong oak flavor, and he looked around the room to see how the others liked it. All avoided his glance, swirling their glasses in front of their faces, looking skyward as they tasted the wine, swallowing hard, as if they had been made to eat a cockroach.

Funny who we are, Paul thought. Why do we like the flavor of wood?

He looked at his wife. She smiled and touched her glass to his to make a toast.

When they got home they realized the worm had emerged a full three inches more. One might draw the conclusion, Paul thought, that exposure of the worm to society actually loosened it, made it come out more.

"Look," Paul said to Valerie, holding the thing across his upper lip. "I can wear it as a mustache."

"Pretty soon you'll be able to wear it as a tie," she said laughing.

"I'll do rope tricks like a cowboy," he said, circling his arm in the air.

The days went by, and still Paul kept feeling like he was forgetting something. He did not return to work but went out in public, to the grocery store, to coffee shops, to museums, to bookstores, to movies. He grew accustomed to the change in the way the world treated him, the newspaper vendor avoiding his eyes, pretending to be busy, saying "Just leave the change on the counter," over his shoulder. Paul admitted to himself that most of all he liked going to the movies.

Paul and Valerie argued over whether he was the victim of discrimination. Suddenly, empty restaurants had no free tables. Taxis were taken. Even a car dealership declined to undertake the transaction of trading in his wife's car. "It's a good thing I'm not looking for a job," he said to her.

"It's not that people treat you the way they do because they don't like you," she said back. "It's just that they are afraid."

"What's the difference?" he said.

Before long the nasal worm-snake descended a foot and a half from Paul's face. Its weight made him hunch somewhat, he sometimes wore it over his shoulders when going out, and it got tangled up in his wife's arms and fell around her neck in the night. It was clear to both of them that it was going to get worse before it got better. Valerie began to wonder what getting better was going to be like.

When the snake was down to his waist, hanging limply and heavily, she told him of her anxiety, knowing a big change was coming but not knowing how it was going to be. He tried to comfort her.

"It looks like this thing is coming all the way out," he said. "So the problem will be solved."

"I want it to happen, Paul, I do. But I have to admit that there's a part of me that just wants that goddamn snake to go back inside and stay there, for things to go back to how they were. We had such a good life, we had it made, and we didn't appreciate it."

"But that's just it—it'll come out, and then we can go back to normal."

"Oh Paul, don't you get it? It's not like that. When it comes all the way out, everything will be different."

"I'll still be me."

She looked at him sympathetically. "Oh Paul," she said, shaking her head. "Paul, Paul, Paul."

He understood.

What else.

One day Paul, carrying his camera, went to the bank and realized that his condition had certain benefits. Because of it, service was accelerated. When he left the bank the red-robed Buddhists monks flocked by him on the sidewalk. Or perhaps it was a different flock of Buddhist monks, he couldn't tell.

Then the second-to-last monk stepped out of the flock and said, "Hello, Mr. Photographer." The monk didn't seem to notice the gigantic worm. Paul smiled and said hello to his old friend. Then he realized that it might not be the same monk. Some time had passed, and it was hard to tell. They all dressed the same, all had shaved heads. "That's quite a coincidence," he said to the monk, testing it out. "Running into you."

"It's not really a coincidence," the monk said.

Whoa, Paul thought to himself. Pay attention this time.

"You see, some of the guys are now making a sand painting at the Buddhist center, which is only four blocks from here." The monk looked back over his shoulder.

"Sand painting?" Paul asked.

"Yes. We make a big painting on a table. But we don't use paint, we use colored sand. Very elaborate. It is a kind of a map."

"A map of what?"

"A map of everything. A map of the universe."

"I guess it's not to scale," Paul said spontaneously, before hoping he hadn't been rude.

The monk smiled. "It is," he said. "Maybe a different scale. Anyway it's very big. It takes days to complete. And when it's done, we wipe it all away."

My goodness, Paul thought. His dilemma came to mind, that life had no meaning because nothing could be accumulated permanently. And here this monk was telling him that they achieved something, and purposefully destroyed it. They celebrated the very thing that drove Paul's mind to desperation.

"You should come see it sometime, before it is wiped away, before it is finished," the monk said. "It's very beautiful."

"I'd like that," Paul said to the monk he may or may not have known. "I've got some free time now, due to my condition." He pointed at the worm. "I suppose you noticed my friend here."

The monk looked at the worm and back at Paul. "Yes," he said. "You are very lucky," the monk said.

"Well," Paul said. "I suppose it doesn't happen to everybody."

"Not right away," the monk said.

"I wonder why not?" Paul said.

And then the monk said, "Once you start a war, it is very difficult to stop."

The following day, Paul and Valerie met at an upscale restaurant, having reserved over the phone so they could not be denied a table when they arrived. The black worm was down to his knee. He carried it in a bag at his side. She was at the restaurant when he got there and hugged him and they sat down at the table. They ordered and started to talk, but Valerie had already sensed something different about Paul.

And that is nearly everything that happened to Paul Sescau. Soon after meeting his wife in the restaurant, Paul Sescau would be gone forever. He was essentially gone already, but had not yet realized it. But I can now tell you the last thing that happened to him.

Over dinner Valerie said to me that she had realized many things in recent days. Things had been hard for me, she said, because civilization was not attuned to this. Civilization was not geared to create it, either, though one might think that was its purpose. In fact, it was taken aback by it, repulsed by it, frightened by it. It was even tempted to try to destroy it, to defend itself.

I then said one of the last things I would ever think wholly rationally.

"Look at how limited our experience is," I said. "Life on earth is the only life we know. If you had an intergalactic business, would you hire an earthling? Would you hire someone so provincial? So—how could you say it—mono-thoughtful?"

Valerie apologized for all I was made to go through. But she also said I should feel sorry for people, really. "I speak from my own experience," she said. "I know the feelings because I've had them myself. You are a reminder of some other life, something we all assumed would happen to us, but then it didn't happen, it doesn't seem to be happening, and we've looked for every way we can to hide from that. It's hard seeing someone like you, someone getting it all out, someone becoming . . . "

I felt something stirring deep inside me then. I was sweating.

"Are you all right?" Valerie asked.

"Yes," I said, gripping the side of the table.

"Don't give up on them, Paul. People will surprise you."

"Well, Val," I said, groaning. "If you can't trust other people with this . . . "

My head hit the table. Valerie hurried to my side, calling my name. I was clenching my gut. She helped me lean back in my chair, and then I staggered to my feet. The people at the tables around us turned in my direction and froze.

"I'm sorry, everyone," I said loudly in a high, comically nasal voice. And then the black worm starting pouring out of my nose, foot after slimy foot, flopping to the floor in a pile. Gasps went up from the other tables. Valerie stood back and watched, her eyes filled with fear. I tried to reassure her, saying "It's nothing, darling," but the worm kept coming. As it fell, its slime splattered the floor around me. Soon my feet were covered in coils of snake. It kept coming, and I could feel it moving brusquely through my head. Seconds passed. It kept coming, but suddenly I could feel pressure releasing in my left nostril. The snake thinned, and its color gradually changed from dark black to bright yellow. The end was coming.

"It's almost out!" I yelled.

"Oh my god!" Valerie said. "What do we do?"

"You gotta keep it from going back in," someone shouted. Valerie turned to him.

"That's right," a woman said. "It'll jump right back in if you're not careful."

And another: "Let's take that thing and flush it down the toilet!"

Others chimed in:

"I don't see how we can get it to the toilet in time."

"We could move him to the toilet."

"But it's too late—"

"There's too much out—"

"It'd take an hour to feed it all down the toilet—"

"Then what do we do?" Valerie said. The yellow snake still flowed out. Looking over the top of it I saw the restaurant manager appear, and soon after, the head chef. The chef looked at me, looked at the deep pile of worm on the floor, and then back at me before disappearing again into the kitchen.

"We got to block his face," someone said. "Try to keep that thing from going back."

Another said, "Okay, but if it wants back in, it's going back in. Those things are as strong as ten men."

"And slippery as all get-out," someone added.

The worm was getting thinner and thinner, until at last it felt as if only dental floss were passing through my nasal passage. The sense of relief from the unplugging was euphoric. I felt as if I was floating. I had this incredibly strong feeling of getting it all out, one complete and final time, an extreme intensification of the relief-freedom you get the moment you pull your caught finger out of a bottle neck. Now everything was popped loose, pulled free, unstuck, jerked out, and the vessel was released clean and free.

The chef appeared again. This time he was armed with a meat cleaver. His staff followed behind him, carrying knives and garbage bins.

"Stand back!" the chef yelled as he and the other cooks plunged into the mounds of black and yellow snake flesh, hacking at it wildly, then sweeping chunks into the bins. They slipped on the red liquid that spurted out, so much like human blood, only thicker and brighter, like in a cheap old vampire movie. Valerie and the other diners joined in, tracking down segments of worm squirming away from the melee, taking over the knifing from the exhausted cooks, carrying filled garbage bins back into the kitchen and emptying them onto blue gas flames turned up to maximum intensity. The employees and the well-dressed customers were all soon clambering around in the slick mass, crawling under tables with their knives, shouting to each other, knocking away chairs, their faces covered with worm flesh, worm slime, worm innards. When the thing was completely out of me, I took my first deep breath in days, surrounded by these strangers who clasped onto me and stood guard should any stretch of worm attempt to reenter my nose.

The place was a wreck. Garbage bins lay here and there, red streaks of worm blood and slime were ground into the carpet, shoes and dishes and cutlery cluttering the floor. The employees and customers were soaked. They checked and rechecked every inch of the restaurant to make sure no worm-snake remained. When everyone finally felt safe, they applauded. They hugged me and each other.

And then I saw something that would have confused Paul Sescau, but doesn't surprise me at all: A number of people approached the table where Valerie and I had been sitting to get a look at what I had been eating.

NOTSEEING (a contemporary vision)

aJbishop

3itemsfromthegrocerybagaftergoldsmith (spinach) épinard bébé/kg ingredients: 162808x emp le 16/01/2011 meil av 21/1/2011. 235 kg 8.00 $1.88 net kg prix totals. bourassa st-sauveur ltée st-sauveur qc iga iga 8507 680 chemin du village morin heights 06-54 (cheese) empaqueté le janv 04, 11 meilleur avant janv 25, 11 poids net kg prix unitaire prix total 0.245 kg $52.89/kg $12.96 gruyère do grotte caved gruyère ingredients: fait de lait cru culture bactérienne sel presure enzyme mg 32% humidity 36% valeur nutritive nutrition facts pour 100 g per 100 g tenure % valeur quotidienne amount & daily value calories/calories 400 lipides/fat 32 g saturés/saturated 19 g + trans fat 15 g 95% cholesterol/cholesterol 100 mg sodium/sodium 600 mg 26% glucides/carbohydrate 0 g 0% fibres/fibre 0 g sucres/sugar 0 g protéines/protein 27 g vitamine A/vitamin A 30% vitamine C/vitamin C 0% calcium/calcium 80% fer/iron 2% (tostitos) new nouveau 0 trans fat 0 gras tran tostitos blue corn maïs bleu fraîcheur garantie guaranteed fresh until printed date jusqu'à la date inclus fe 1 515333113 56 1: 52 tostitos salsa medium moyenne the goodness of blue corn les bienfaits du maïs bleu 250 g chips tortilla chips we use real blue corn to make our uniquely delicious tostitos blue corn tortilla chips is there such a thing as blue corn there are several varieties of corn including yellow white and blue and the colour of tostitos blue corn tortilla chips comes naturally from the kernel so there are no artificial colours or flavours for more information on blue corn visit tostitos.ca nous utilisons du vrai maïs bleu pour fabriquer nos delicieuses chips tortilla maïs bleu tostitos le maïs bleu existe-t-il vraiment absoluement il existe differentes variétés de maïs dont le jaune le blanc et le bleu et les chips tortilla maïs bleu de tostitos tirent naturellement leur couleurs de leurs grains ces chips tortilla ne contiennent donc aucun colorant ni arôme artificiel pour en savoir plus sur le maïs bleu visitez le site tostitos.ca

tostitos salsa medium moyenne suggested serving presentation suggéré
what makes tostitos blue corn tortilla chips even better new tostitos best
ever salsa made with vine ripened tomatoes fresh onions zest jalapeno
peppers and just a touch of _____ boring boring—it is in-
teresting to note what we do not see—bombarded by textual stimuli it is
necessary to shut down—to frame—to edit—to protect—to manage—
not seeing is disturbed so that remedial seeing happens—what is also
notseen is the pile-up of bodies in the world news broadcasts and the
one-armed guy at the bottom of the escalator guy/concordia metro and
the billboards on the 15 autoroute north and south which present dis-
tractions from a line of red lights bordering on mesmerizing at 120 k/
hour—   Notseeing:

> the ability to think of what is not[1]—what is out
> of fingertip and eye range uncoloured
> and not smelt and not held against
> a surveyor's glass and carpenter's level[2]
> un-leveled by any shadow cave[3] imprint
> or otherwise tracing and trapping[4]
> called En Sof by those who made
> mystic trees of not knowing
> and by those who made not proving
> a virtue woven in mind's sternum eye
> conjured in mantra breathing and burning[5]

---

1. Sartre. (God died and went to imagination)?
2. Only love, He says to his twelve, is the great leveller.
3. Can this glorious, earthly life be a mere cave on which the shadows of reality play for me in my mind's reach, gaining lugubrious ground with silhouettes parched from a radiance that is beyond the lip of the cave entrance, and me entranced by shadows? Plato, how did you not despair with such an imagination for what could be?
4. Do not be deluded by the promise of certainty: Think of how Gregory of Nyssa, so long ago, warned us of the demise of the quest when too quickly we assume the truth. Think of Bergson who, not so long ago, made death the consequence of fact. Am I paraphrasing from my own fears of being trapped in arrogance? Do I prefer chaos to stasis?
5.   . . . Forget phraseology.
    I want burning, burning.
            Be friends
    with your burning. Burn up your thinking
    and your forms of expression.
            – Rumi

words sung upward against
the current[6] until splits unseal the soul[7]
spilling all un-matter
in meaningful waves across an invisible
horizon[8] mixing endless unknowing[9]

---

6. Floodwaters pour from a reasoned lineage [vii], linking us so that speech and highways function and something like cooperation happens. But why is it dangerous to dive under into silence where the waterfall's source can be known as if from above? Only to keep small what could be boundless [viii]. Imagine if everyone could swim there!

7. Imagined in *The Zohar,* by Abraham Abulafia (1240–1291), who wandered from Spain to the near East to sew little threads along the mystical way, from Kabbalah to the Pope to the Tibetan Buddhists to the future in psychoanalytics — teaching how to go beyond normal consciousness and discover a new world.

8. Do you feel the horizon in the longing to be bigger than you are, to see outside conventional reach [ix] and to grasp what is sometimes spoken of in whispers by those who are afraid of the people who claim to know?

9. But nevertheless somehow, somewhere, some way, known.

THE POISONOUS MUSHROOM

Catie Jarvis

God is a bulky bear-like creature with long furry arms and an admirably large head. I am cooing on the floor, soft and warm as everything around me. There is a pulsing heat, which *is* me, a radiant star among other stars. Pick your shape, God commands, or tries to. His voice is tired and doesn't carry far.

We are on a veranda overlooking a white passage, a kind of highway, where there is a constant bustle of those headed in and out. It's the same place we've been meeting for a long time, although time here is irrelevant and unaccounted for. Down on the road of wandering souls, a butterfly passes, wings spanning gold and green across the world's blank background, in a hurry, it seems, to see an old companion from an old world. Near the butterfly trots a broad black horse and an attractive woman holding hands with a man in a cap. The woman dresses in a fabric that I don't understand, succulent, thick, and glowing. I look for my own hand, with which I want to touch the strange fabric, but I am nothing yet but a ball of light; I can sense my own glow.

Choose anything, God says, sweeping his paw across the scene before us. He points to a fluffy cat. He points to a tall pine tree. You can do better than them, my dear. Show me what you're made of!

I try to snarl from the bottom of my throat, though at this moment I have none.

God moves closer to me, tilting his big brown bear eyes. He caresses the air around me, an enticing touch, which apologizes like a strayed lover. Despite the heat I coil coldly, and as he pulls away I choose my form and stand.

My right arm hangs off the joint, dislocated and limp. I rest it on my coarse and hairy legs, covered in red lesions from unsanitary conditions. I still feel at home in this body. God gives me chance after chance to start again from nothing, to choose differently, but it always ends up the same. I run my left hand through my hair and feel for the patches where it has thinned; they are there, they assure me. My tattered shirt is a-mix with feces, blood, and bile, though I cannot smell them. There's no smell here. My face stands out gaunt, pale and blotchy, so different than the smooth pure faces that surround me. With thin, parched lips I smile towards God, showing him the gap of my three missing teeth.

You mean to punish me still? God asks but doesn't wait for an answer. He is used to ruling. He says, I know the reason for all events and their outcome. You can't convince me otherwise. You can't defeat me!

He does this sometimes, grows arrogant.

I spit in his furry face, my saliva yellow and toxic.

I wish you had brushed your teeth, says God.

And so do I.

God wipes the spit away and sits at our small white table on our small white veranda and sighs. Won't you tell me a story? He asks.

I pull my book out of its satchel, so dull and dark compared to this world. I place it on the table, but it falls through to the ground; the table is not equipped to hold such an object. Piece of crap, God says, slamming his fist down. I pick up the book and place it on my lap. God runs his fingers over the cover, and I swear it's like he remembers being just a man, alive, sitting in some study engrossed in words and pages. I would never tell him of this suspicion. That is not part of his story.

The cover of the book, my book, is forest green, an entirely earthly color. At its center, the caricatured face of a man melds with the rounded stem of a mushroom. The man's head is topped with a spotted mushroom hat. A red beard hangs around his neck and a gold star of David adorns his mushroom chest. Behind him, other smaller mushroom men—interestingly all of them are men—pop up from the ground and peek at the reader. These men have bulbous noses and droopy, downtrodden eyes. This cover once appeared to me grotesque and maddening. But I have altered its messages and made it my own, and now, I am merely nostalgic.

God touches the star on the mushroom, and his finger lingers upon it.

It's the only book there was, I tell God. The only thing with pages, pictures, or words. Such a precious combination. I coveted that book. I read it to my daughter every night, always a different story, always a kinder story.

Der Giftpilz, I'd say, *The Toadstool.*

I'd ask my daughter: do you know what it means to be a toadstool?

Poisonous to your enemies, she would say, clever and strong and impossible to ingest!

You taught her well, says God.

I shake my head, no. She was too young for the lessons she learned.

I look up to see that God is now as muscular as a Greek warrior. He is adorned with twinkling jewels, a golden necklace, an amber crown, a loin cloth.

I am on the floor again, awaiting my form, a chance to come alive anew. It has been hours or days or years since the last time, there is no way of knowing anything but that this has happened before and that it will happen again.

What will you be, Sarah? He asks of me.

His voice is more sure as a Greek God than as a bear. But I assume the same form again.

It's odd, says God, your unhappiness.

I run my hand across my leg and wipe some brown goop from my ankle. It may be dirt or shit. I reach out and rub it on God's shiny chest.

Why don't you go back and live through what I've lived through and then we'll talk, I say rashly.

But I live through all of mankind, God says with a charring Greek-God laugh.

You live through it here? I ask. Like this? I say, eyeing his elaborate costume. I look down at my hands that are scarred across the protruding bones, dehydrated like the skin of a woman much older, cut around the cuticles and dirty beneath the nails. God's manicured hands stroke his silky rope nervously as if they know they are being watched. I often make him fidgety.

We sit down at our table on the veranda. There is more traffic than usual today. A buzz rises from the hubbub, though no actual sound emanates. We communicate through our thoughts; no noise is necessary.

Tell me about it then, Sarah. Show me how you saw.

Lager 1, I tell him, is moated and fenced. We fill its small barracks with our grey narrow bodies striped with pus like gold. Our eyes are so accustomed to seeing blood that they drown themselves in red. A subversive act we all hope to survive.

I am drawn to faces; it is my way. A person cannot see his own face, but a stranger can. And so I always take care to notice. I consider this my occupation and trick myself into believing that this is why I can do it . . . I clean up after the kill, like a hunter's only child, but there are many of us, hundreds taking wheelbarrows to the pits in shifts. Some think of them as corpses. Some turn away. I look closely at chins and eyelids. I try to recall the way they stare or the position of their lips in order to preserve them in some small way—their last observation.

I am never afraid of these dead or dying bodies, not even of their blood and vomit which draws the flies. My dead still hold traces of love in their frozen eyes, beneath the pores of their bald scalps, between gold tooth and gum as we pull out this last treasure from flesh, anyplace where one might protect it.

It is the living faces of the Nazi men that frighten me. They talk vacantly. They stare up towards the sky, afraid to look at the ground and what they have done to it. I know that I will die, sometimes I hope for it. And though it is a strange idea that I could perish as a vessel, lose my means of impacting the world, it is less strange than the notion that creatures like our captors could live on.

Show me one of these men, God asks. I have not seen one up close, for obvious reasons.

I've never talked about this part of my life, God, not to anyone. I didn't have the chance to.

But there's no hesitation within you, he tells me.

He's right. I feel so free. It is a beautiful freedom and I am momentarily thankful for it, momentarily filled with a feeling that I might call grace.

A man, they called him Michael, stands before the victims in a white coat. He tells the lies each time with the exact same words, the same pitch and intonation. "Be calm. There is nothing to fear here. You will soon be sent to work. First, you will remove all clothes and belongings to bathe and disinfect." He wakes up each day with these words. He remembers them and repeats them.

The more I hear his speech echoing through the doors of the death chamber, the more afraid I grow of people who stick to wording, who recite from passages without thinking first, without feeling.

Religious men you mean?

Not exactly . . .

Believers?

Yes, believers. Michael believes in every word. He believes in his cause, and he believes that because of his convictions he has the right to rob others of their beliefs, of their lives. Michael's coat is long, neat, and sterile like his words. I would rather him mimic the burning vocal chords of the men and women and children who scream so loud and thick that I almost wish for their silence. It would be better than his neatness and his practiced phrases. It would be better than his acceptance that each day the mess will be cleaned and he will begin again without changing a single word. How can any person accept this?

How? How? Asks God delightedly, like a child demanding the long awaited answer to a riddle.

You don't understand, I explain, the question is rhetorical. Unless *you* have the answer?

Oh. I see. I am still getting used to this.

Why do you come here with me? I ask God.

It feels Socratic. Socrates was tired of talking by the time I met him. He takes form as solid immovable objects. He might be this table. God bangs on the table and calls, Socrates, are you in there?

I've always longed for discourse, God says, for culture.

Why don't you just create some?

I have, Sarah. I have made great cultures; I rule and reign over them all! God stands with this declaration and his toga slips off, drops to the floor. Surprisingly, he is sterile underneath his robe: Flat, smooth, genderless as a doll. He doesn't bother to pull up his robe. Unashamed, he sits down again beside me and leaves the cloth there at his feet.

You're missing something there, I say, and point towards his lower half.

Oh, yes, I have been forgetful lately.

Sterile and cultureless; how sad.

Yes, Sarah. It is my greatest sadness, God says. But there can't be culture here. Happiness is naked. It's as pure and uninteresting as talking to a newborn. There's one over there, he points below us to a puppy dog happily traipsing along. Died after one week. Must have seen another puppy and recalled the image as a joyful one.

How can you tell he lived so briefly? I ask.

The newborn thinks only *I exist! I exist!* over and over in different ways. They know it better than anyone, but it is all that they know.

Like you, I say.

God doesn't like this, but he lets it slide.

Read me the book, God demands.

I take out my object, this one thing that came here with me, though God and I still can't quite figure how. That it's a part of my soul is his explanation. But how can it be? An old book with worn pages, propaganda from another time and world: How can such a thing attach itself to something as ethereal as a soul?

God, still Greek and muscular, leans into me as I pull the book into the bright light of his world. I fear God would stare at my book forever if I let him. I know it can't be good for him, can't be right. Sometimes I'm afraid that I'm having a poor effect on him. Forgetting to finish his own genitalia . . . what will be next?

Once upon a time, I read to God, a boy and his mother set out into the forest on a sunny summer day to gather mushrooms for their dinner. They are so free, this boy and his mother, that they can set out at any time, return home at any time, and eat all the mushrooms that they want! But in every peaceful world there lurks danger.

I stop and hold the book to my bony chest.

I can feel my daughter's cheek pressing into my shoulder. At this part in the story she would close her eyes and imagine being in a plush green forest, imagine being so free.

Show the book here, God says. Stop hogging it.

I turn the picture book towards him and continue.

The mother and son spot some mushrooms in the forest, I say. Some of these mushrooms are smooth and bright, while others look dingy, dirty, and trampled upon.

Just like these mushrooms, the mother says to her son, people can either be good or bad. They start off as innocent seeds but as they grow up different things affect them. Rain and drought, sun and cold, the whispers of the mushrooms around them, the fear instilled by predators passing by. For these reasons some mushrooms end up being good, just as some people end up being good. Some mushrooms end up being poisonous, bad mushrooms, like some people grow to be bad. We have to be wary of poisonous people just as we have to be wary of bad mushrooms. Do you understand?

The boy nods in reply. Being involved with dangerous people could be just like eating a poisonous mushroom. It could kill you! The boy exclaims.

And here my daughter would shudder. She saw death. She knew its face, its name, its result.

I would stop the book here, I tell God. Close it and hide it. My daughter was not to see the remaining pages and the poison they spoke. Not ever. I would finish the story in my own way, differently each time. And at the end of my story, I would take my daughter's hand. We each have a choice in our life, I would tell her, to be good or bad, kind or malicious. Sometimes it can be an easy choice and other times it can be very hard. We must decide whether to poison those who we think wrong us or to forgive them.

Yes, Mother, she would say, I can see that.

And which do you choose? I would ask my daughter.

What did she say? God asks eagerly.

I sigh. No matter how many times I asked her this same question, she could never decide.

God is an enormous dragonfly with beady black bug eyes on either side of his head. He's mating incessantly with another giant dragonfly. Their wings are long and glow in brilliant shades of orange and green.

I am an orb on the floor.

Choose a form, God casually suggests. Perhaps he has given up on me. Perhaps this will be our last conversation, and he will find some other lost souls to amuse him from now on.

I come into my chosen form and begin to limp away from him.

Come back, Sarah, he calls after me.

I can't talk while you're doing that.

Okay. Okay.

He shoos his companion away.

Tell me how you died, Sarah. Maybe then we can move past this hideous container you keep choosing to parade about in.

I won't release it.

Tell me anyway, says God.

Fine, I bark, but then pause for a drawn moment, making God wait. In our silence I am reminded of a stubbornness from my childhood, the way I would wait until the very last minute to rise from bed for school, as if by waiting beyond my mother's soft morning kiss, and then waiting still beyond her yells from the kitchen and threats of punishment, I was somehow making the waking my own. I have not thought of my childhood, before the war, for a very long time.

I can see God growing impatient and take one moment more to relish in his frustration before I begin.

On the day that I die, I have eyes sunken in and shaded rosy-brown, a jaw so tight to skin it almost snaps with every word I whisper in the night, I tell God. When I sleep, I feel my hip bones digging into the floor and wake up bruised by the thinness of my own flesh. I am too weak to work, and I know well what is coming.

God takes my hand with his wing, and we walk together down from our veranda and amongst the other beings on the passage. There is a great deal of movement, souls always wandering here and there. I would have expected this place to be more calm and static, but even full of tranquility, these beings cannot seem to sit still.

I walk the Road to Heaven, I explain to God. This is what the Nazis named it. The Road to Heaven winds through a painted corridor. Painted with a rich and lovely mural of a dense green forest, thick, healthy, brown trees and bushy evergreens. My daughter is by my side and I whisper to her. This is the forest where we pick our mushrooms and eat them until we are so very full. This is our forest where we learn that the difference between good and evil is all in how we look at the world, where we learn to love everything whether it is good or bad. This, I tell her, is the forest where we go to be free.

Some of the beings that surround me and God have paused to listen. A tall man. A shadowy ghost. A stout and wormy pig. They stare at me, curiously and kindly. Perhaps they have never heard a story like this before. I wonder what they looked like in their previous lives and what has compelled them to choose their forms. I wonder how they can manage to stare so peacefully. As I continue with my story, I entertain the possibility of enraging them with my words, of an uprising.

The Nazi's uniform is collared and booted, with red armbands. Your uniform, God, is creative and varied. We who die here have a uniform as well. Ours is nakedness. But it is not a pure nakedness, not like babies or angels. We are sharp in different ways, bruised and scabbed like violent artwork calling out and declaring our presence while we still can. Our uniform is our thin starving bodies, our bald heads. Our uniform is our knowledge of evil and the strength it takes to endure it. We can still feel, even now, when we know for sure that no one will save us.

The forest mural leads into the chamber. The chamber is decorated with golden prairie flowers and a large golden Star of David. The flowers and the star are a mockery. A false comfort. Despite all of our suffering, we did not ask to die.

God tilts his thin bug antenna down and stops beside me. I sense that he is feeling my death just as I am. I am infuriated by his sadness.

Do you want to know the rest of the story in this book that I carry with me, this object that you say is part of my soul? I ask him, maliciously. Do you want to know the part I never read you, the part I never read my daughter? Do you want to know the moral of this story, its purpose?

God nods.

The moral of the story is that the Nazi boys and girls must come to recognize the hair, the nose, the skin of the Jew. They must know every detail of our shape so that they can make us shapeless, make us monsters of skin and bone, beat us down to the lowest form, so that they may rise up above us. So that they may stomp on us like mushrooms in the forest. It is not a story of good versus evil, but one of dominance.

And, *you*, God, your story is the same! I pick up my book and throw it down beside God, a fragile dragonfly on the ground. His gigantic wings shudder, and I wonder if it's from the force of the hard cover book landing beside them, or from fear.

You're like a sleazy politician running for office, using the whole world as your campaign. You show us evil so that we will still have the desperate need to believe in you. As long as we are scared of each other and of our own selves, then you can control us. As long as we are scared, we will need you. The Nazi is your example of what man can be without your guidance: The devil in human form.

I lift my foot to squash God's beady bug head onto the perfect whiteness of his world. We shall see who the mushroom is now, I think, as I begin to bear my weight down upon him.

Stop, God asks meekly.

Despite how strongly I desire to destroy him, I am compelled to listen. He can be quite persuasive, even as a dragonfly. I pull my foot away from him slowly. He flies up from the ground and hovers there before me.

As our eyes meet, the buzzing begins. It comes from within me and spreads like a bomb or a sound. I swear I can hear it, the buzzing. I realize how much I have missed the sense of sound, that inundation from the outside world, the waves hitting my flesh but not stopping, the sound continuing on for others to hear.

I'm buzzing and buzzing. I watch as my book begins to vibrate on the ground. I reach for it desperately, but it slips from my fingers, falls without a sound, and is absorbed away into nothingness. The sound grows in magnitude, expanding through me in every direction. There is nothing else inside me now but the sound.

God reaches out a giant wing, green like a tropical sea. He hugs it around me and finally I am warm. I am a dragonfly, and I have no means to control or escape my transformation. God grabs my head with his anal claspers and my abdomen bends around so that we are making love mid-flight in the shape of a heart.

Sarah, God says, I will miss you.

FROM HERE TO THE MOON

Olga Zilberbourg

Toward the end of his two-week vacation to Europe, Kevin grew inconsolable. On his last day in London it rained, as it had all four days he'd spent there, but he didn't want to leave. Under the soft drizzle, Kevin toured the London Dungeon, rode the London Eye four hundred feet above the Palace of Westminster, saw the complete Shakespeare in 90 minutes. He could never have his fill of steak and kidney pies, kebabs and curries, glitzy West End shows, and the scene at clubs on the River Thames. The thought of getting on a plane in twelve hours and returning home felt like a defeat. Monday morning he had to put on scrubs and report for duty at the mental health facility where he'd been working for a year since completing his degree in nursing. Monday night he would be sitting at his dad's bedside in the nursing home, watching some dumb reality show.

Kevin returned to his hostel just before midnight. The room was dark and smelled vaguely of iodine and cherry soda. Kevin's roommate, a nineteen-year-old Frenchman, wasn't back yet. Kevin didn't expect him back for hours. He plopped on the bed, turned on the overhead TV, and took out his purchases from the corner shop: a carton of chocolate chip ice cream and a quart of whiskey. He found an old movie playing on one of the BBC channels. Recognizing a young Michael Caine, he turned up the volume. There was no spoon in the room, so he ate the ice cream with the pocketknife he carried in his backpack from his Boy Scout days.

Just as Kevin was catching on to the premise of the movie, a bright light flooded his room from outside. The stains on the rug and the bedspreads stood out as if under black light: that spot by the door where Kevin had spilled half a bottle of rum and soda the other day; the dents in the wall where previous tenants must've banged their heads against the cheap plaster. Working at the mental health facility, Kevin knew just how many psychotic episodes involved people banging their heads against walls. He had started to wonder whether the action brought them some relief.

The light grew brighter, then dimmed—collapsed into a single beam—and an alien stepped into Kevin's room. It wasn't really an alien, of course, but a hologram projection of one. The alien wore a baseball cap that said PITTSFORD COFFEE ROASTERS, a ratty polo shirt, and baggy brown khakis. He had a considerable paunch, but in all other ways looked like an older brother Kevin didn't have. The way Kevin knew the thing was an alien was because it dangled on a beam of light that came from the window. The alien light shimmered beautifully, beating even the view of Paris from the Eiffel Tower.

"Hi, Kev," the alien said. "What's up?"

"Hi," said Kevin, and because his breath was caught in his throat, the only other thing he could say was, "Wow."

"Relax," the alien said. "How about a garbage plate?"

The alien held out a paper plate piled high with home fries and macaroni salad, then topped with two hamburger patties doused in meat sauce, and covered with two pieces of thickly buttered sourdough bread. In Kevin's hometown of Rochester, New York, going out for garbage plates was a pastime for him and his buddies. They drove all the way out to Gates in the middle of the night, smoked joints in the parking lot, and competed for who could finish a plate faster. The food the alien was thrusting at Kevin had no smell and looked inedible. Kevin wondered if this was because it was a hologram projection, or if after two weeks in Europe, he had completely lost his taste for hometown cuisine. He shook his head.

"No? You're missing out!" The alien worked the plastic fork to cut a piece of hamburger and scooped it with some home fries into his mouth. "I'm starving," he said, chewing vigorously. Kevin noticed that the alien's voice sounded like a deep, guttural version of his own voice, as if somebody had recorded him some early morning and was now playing the track back.

As if from the effort of chewing, the alien grew a little staticky; his color faded in and out. He adjusted settings on his watch, and the color came back more brilliant than before, though now his face had a pronounced blue tint. Kevin wondered how much time the alien had on Earth.

"What's your mission?" Kevin asked. "Will you—Do you want to take me with you?"

The alien belched. "Okay," he said, "here's the deal: you've got to stay the course."

"You mean, I should go back to Rochester tomorrow?"

"No, I mean, keep at it."

"The nursing? Well, what else would I do?"

The alien waved his hands in the air in a perfect imitation of Kevin's mother's gesture for *Stop it, stupid*. "Your blueprints for a time machine. Don't give up. Hang tough!"

"A time machine? What time machine?"

The alien winked at him with a conspiratorial look that reminded Kevin of his dad. Until recently, when his dad started to develop dementia, his parents had owned a used bookstore, and Kevin grew up reading old paperback novels. When Kevin was little, he had dreamed of being a scientist or an engineer and working for NASA, and his dad encouraged him by helping him build model planes and write simple computer code. As Kevin grew up, the plots of the novels he was reading started to repeat themselves, and he realized he didn't really have a head for math. But his dad kept on bringing him science magazines and novels about robots and intergalactic travel from the store anyway.

The alien took his cap off, flexed the brim, then slapped it on his head backwards, a gesture that Kevin himself might perform to fill an awkward pause in a conversation. He remembered Pittsford Coffee Roasters, the garage business across the street from his parents' store that had polluted the neighborhood with the smell of burnt coffee. The owner had a habit of forcing his merchandize on all of his neighbors, and Kevin and his parents each owned several identical hats.

Seeing the alien caricature people and places he knew annoyed Kevin. It dawned on him that the alien wanted Kevin to think that it really *was* an older version of himself, come from the future to cheer him on. The attempt was absurd. The human gestures and speech were too perfect, making it obvious that whoever controlled the projection was not a native Earthling. Kevin noted the alien was balding under the cap and wondered if that was characteristic of its species, or if it was a sign of things to come for his own body.

"So I'm supposed to build a time machine?"

The alien nodded cheerfully. "You got it!"

"But how? What am I supposed to do?"

The hologram flickered and spiked, starting to fade.

"Tell me!" Kevin begged. "Don't leave me hanging!"

"Give it time!" The alien made a show of fooling with the settings on his watch, but he continued to grow thinner and more transparent.

Kevin shook his head, trying to organize his thoughts. He didn't buy it about the time machine, not at all. There must've been some mistake, a miscalculation on the alien's part. The alien research department had malfunctioned and messed up everything from the alien's looks to his spiel. The situation felt as sad and embarrassing as when his dad, at a family dinner at Ruby Tuesday shortly before he had to be moved to the nursing home, suddenly forgot how to use a fork and, holding it in his hand, smiled and shook his head, as if marveling at the complexity of its design.

"Am I having a mental breakdown?" Kevin wondered out loud.

"Don't give up," the alien whispered. "Stay the course!"

The moment the alien vanished completely, the room rolled with overwrought music, and Michael Caine's voice boomed from the television, "What are you doing?"

Kevin lowered the volume and discovered that the ice cream in his lap had gone soft. He could squeeze it directly from the tub into his mouth. After a couple of mouthfuls, Kevin gagged and almost threw up. He tossed the creamy puddle into the trashcan and focused on the whiskey. He swigged from the bottle in what he thought was a smooth move, but the whiskey splattered all over his face. Kevin was angry. The notion that he could invent a time machine was preposterous. He didn't need to know college physics—which he'd failed three times—to understand that time travel was theoretically impossible. Whether the apparition had been a dream or a psychotic episode, his innermost nightmares were now revealed in the form of a cheesy, two-bit alien. What a joke!

Early the next morning, his French roommate stumbled in, and the racket he made trying to get his clothes off woke Kevin up. "Je suis désolé," the Frenchman said. "Je suis désolé," he repeated before he finally dropped off to sleep, and Kevin thought, I, too, am desolate. It was time to go to the airport. Kevin's head hurt, and the ice cream had given him a toothache. But when he finally sat up and was able to see the room clearly in the pale morning light, an unsettlingly hopeful feeling moved in his chest.

Kevin found he actually longed to be back at the nursing home, in the room with his father. His father's mind was now mostly blank, but he could still express familiar emotions: bewilderment, hunger, pleasure from being touched. For the past year, Kevin had been grieving the loss of what his father had once been, and yet his father was still there, in Rochester. A version of him persisted. And the recollection of the alien heartened Kevin: a potential self, and not without a sense of humor, waiting for him.

Kevin took a shower and packed his bag, working calmly and steadily, while London stood like a witness, blurry-eyed, outside. This morning he felt slightly less foreign. He'd be back before too long.

bacche kā pōtRā

LaTasha N. Nevada Diggs

bloom, the dandelion dance of Keisha's mane. a Wave
of bush. her kitchen pearls & truffula treetops.
begin the traction. tug. creamy crack. lye ale. wave

so long. mares can be jumpy. but baby-girl's plumes burnt.
crunchy bacon. her puberty looms early. fizzled particles
stuck to a flat iron. diapers don't detect ovarian cysts. wave

adieu corkscrew. the follicles doomed. scorched sirens—
coils use to protect from ultraviolet. all for a ponytail? wave
to trichologist mama. to groom was spiritual once. now gray
pus from scalp drench tissue. lingering, a caustic perfume.

"bacche kā pōtRā" is a golden shovel which is a recent poetic form created by Terrance Hayes based on a Gwendolyn Brooks poem. The title of the poem is Hindi/Urdu for nappy. The poem contains the line "wave treetops wave burnt particles wave sirens wave gray perfume" from the poem "eleven maroons," written by Fred Moten.

ESTANCADOS :: ATASCADA

Jordan Reynolds

After "Ballad of the Little Girl Who Invented the Universe"

Now there are more infrared sensors
that tell me *I love you* to the sound of applause.

My flexible eyes lull. Bilingual mouthfuls dribble
holy stillness, presents asked for are received.

Saturday's girlishness teaches the history
of Czech jazz combos and the charred wreckage

of the HMS *Nancy*, 1814. The actual cause
of my being stuck is this dirty heart. Last night

we got along fairly well in Victor's coat.
Hey, there are thousands of ways to listen,

and still unknown information, like the sequence
B-U-E-A-Y-O-A-O-B: *no results found.*

The fan club for the next President sent
the diagram for power flow to his scouts.

There is still some profit to be made.
A small advantage.

A Note on Progressive Translation

In his lecture "Poetry and Politics," Jack Spicer stated "fundamentally a poem comes from the Outside." The poem above, "Estancados :: Atascada," comes from a collection of progressive translations in progress and is a response to and dialogue with Spicer's concept of poet-as-receiver and his book *After Lorca*. I use a system of invention that introduces static in each iteration of the process and mostly refuses the poet's involvement in choosing language. This produces poems that are fundamentally *received* (via the process).

To produce these translations, I do the following:

1. I read Spicer's poem into an iPhone application called Dragon Naturally Speaking that turns speech into text. The software is set to listen for Spanish words, so reading Spicer's English (literally *dictated*) into it produces garbled Spanish. For example, a line from "Ballad of the Little Girl Who Invented the Universe" becomes:

> Ahora todo lo que ha dado cuenta entreteniendo más sensores infrarrojos te amo

2. I then run the Spanish text through Google Translate and turn it into garbled English. In this step, arbitrary syntactic and linguistic connections emerge:

> Now all he has noticed more infrared sensors entertaining
> I love you

3. From these two drafts, I create an "enhanced" version. I reference dictionaries and various online and in-print resources to make connections and insert this information into a new draft. To investigate proper names and places that surface in the versions, I typically use a simple Google search and pull information at-random from the results. An example from this stage:

> It [is/are/be] makes the [also: does the] eyes are loose for
> [to please/on behalf of] Flex leave for [to go back] San

[Saint] Mam [WIKIPEDIA: people of Guatemala who typically speak Spanish and Mam (a Mayan dialect)] snack [a bite: a mouthful] bag made [presented, filed, introduced, showed] me reject for them when stuck [stagnant, stalled]

4. Finally, I re-read Spicer's poem as a guide for tone/form/sound, and then work through multiple versions of each line/group of lines. I then write my final poem, collecting nuances from the Spanish and English versions and leaving intact as much of the original dictated language and syntax as possible.

In her recent book of essays, *Madness, Rack, and Honey*, Mary Ruefle states that "a poem must rival physical experience and metaphor is, simply, an exchange of energy between two things." The process of making these poems forces matter and energy into each line via chance, not to mention the literal energy transfers taking place between the various software involved. The arrival of the HMS *Nancy*, for instance, is not something Spicer would have expected, but it's somehow there in the work, as are Victor, the President, and Czech jazz combos. The resulting kenosis affirms the particulate nature of our existence. That these various phenomena can exist within the same space is a testament to the power of the poem (not to the power of the poet), an idea I think Spicer would find amenable.

In addition to the generation of static—and the instillation of a peculiar patience in the process of making each poem—these translations also build community with Spicer, Federico García Lorca, and the various ghosts that unexpectedly haunt the poems. William Butler Yeats (whose spooks brought him metaphors for his own poems) encountered this, as did James Merrill and his group of friends and fellow poets gathered around their Ouija board. These translations (in Spicer's words) "give messages to the poet, [and] to other poets." My voice interacts with Spicer's, but also spirals outwards to interact with others: the process (and the language) spirals in both directions indefinitely.

2020

Erin Fitzgerald

When I was small, my father and I had a room at the compound. It was a nice room, painted, with a window and a soft, dark-blue rug on the floor. I was on a scavenge team and I found plates, blankets, and socks for us. My father mostly went on rounds with my aunt. She visited the sick and took notes for the compound doctor to read at the end of the day. My father talked to the women of the sick. He managed their little tasks. He held their hands. He comforted them. Sometimes they came to us and stayed overnight. Sometimes he returned to our room in the morning, after curfew. One of those times was when he brought the rug.

One afternoon I came home and my aunt was in our room. She was as direct with me as she was with the sick. "Your father had to leave," she said. "You're to come live with me."

I went to gather some things, but she shook her head. "Best to start over."

I still dream about the rug.

Sometimes I sold a toaster I'd managed to rewire, or before curfew I'd break into a car and there would be a first aid kit in the glove box. In those ways, I earned enough credit for an hour of electricity. I brought out the box that plays videotapes, and I switched out the wiring from the box that plays discs. I ignored the hot, sharp smell when I flipped the switch, and there it was, on our television—a school where everything was clean, in a sunny town with pools just for swimming, with mail for sending love notes, and endless plates and trays of food.

It was beautiful everywhere on the television, but I watched the students the most. They were immaculate. I watched the twins who don't look at all alike, and the girl who I thought was a woman in secret. But I looked at Dylan the most. His hair was crafted like a holiday meal. His clothes were darker than the others, more subdued. He often propped himself up against a wall and tried to look indifferent. With a little coaching Dylan could live with us, with me.

When the electricity is cut off, there is always a little latent spark still in the wire, an invisible cloud of heat. I breathed it in, and took it with me for evening chores. Here's how to boil laundry, I murmured. Here's how to stare down a sight into the dark. I felt Dylan at my elbow, paying attention to the lessons I gave, the information I shared. If I could have seen Dylan's truest face, or even his most calculated gaze, it would be warm, like a happy sun.

Most evenings, my aunt came back to our room after I did. I helped her take off her shoes and socks while I told her about the weather. A slow sadness in the morning, but happy in the afternoon. Its temper rose as I'd finished my scavenging for the day, and I'd raced home against it.

She glanced out our tiny window, at the dark grey flashing clouds. "Still angry out now," she said. "What did you find today?"

I showed her a wool sweater, two jars of relish, half a bottle of fabric softener.

"Very nice," she said. "That's two weeks' rent, easy. Maybe I'll rest my feet tomorrow!"

I didn't show her the batteries or the pocket knife. I didn't show her the key ring that looks like a little license plate with my own name on it.

My aunt motioned for me to close the window more, so the rain didn't come in.

My favorite mornings were the bright happy ones where I stood on a street corner with seven other kids and waited for my assignments.

There were dead leaves everywhere, and new weeds pushed up the sidewalks in all of our neighborhoods. Before I went to live with my aunt, I had worked on a crew where we had four hours to toss four houses, and sometimes they'd hide things to make sure we did it right. The new crew didn't worry about electric wires on the ground. They gave out a bonus if I brought back my garbage bags dry, with no rips. They only checked our pockets and socks, and not our underwear.

When I got too big to crawl through basement windows, they told me to stay home.

—ɯ—

I found a new job in the kitchen because my aunt changed the compound cook's mother's bedding in the infirmary, and she remembered to smooth out the wrinkles in the blankets. My father had taught me how to cook when I was small, while he was making meals for his friends who had stayed overnight.

By the end of my first week in the kitchen, I'd showed the cook how to make bread that was easier to chew. The cook looked like the blond man who was Dylan's friend, who always smiled with his mouth but never his eyes. The cook held the steel door open for me at the curfew-warning whistle, and put his arm around my shoulders as he pulled it shut after us.

"You are the littlest miracle," he said.

My aunt bought me thirty minutes of electricity when she came home, to celebrate. She watched it with me.

Dylan had two girlfriends who were identical except for their hair. Sometimes they didn't get along. They yelled and cried and he pushed them and kissed them to quiet them. My aunt knitted bandages while they asked him to choose which of them he loved more. He drank beer in bottles by himself and threw them, and didn't clean up the mess.

"He deserves whatever comes to him," my aunt said. "Just like my brother."

My aunt said things like that sometimes. I always pretended I didn't hear her, because it was just the two of us in the room with no rug.

"They should ask him who he loves more when it's raining," I said. "That's what matters the most."

My aunt laughed so hard that she coughed, and I had to bring her water.

I wouldn't make Dylan choose. I would ask him what he thinks about when he wants to fall asleep. I would agree with him that I'm tired of hearing about before the weather had moods, when people lived hundreds of miles away from each other for no reason, when you could hurt yourself from eating too much. I would fill a brown bottle with whiskey and I would drink it like he does, pointing the bottom at whatever came to us next.

"I watch you knead that bread of yours," the cook said. "And my shoulders ache so much. "

None of us should have to choose. But I would love Dylan most when the sadness lifts from the ground in the mornings.

My aunt collapsed in the infirmary. I visited her when I could.

The cook told me he'd made a roast pigeon to take to her. He wouldn't let me take it until I sat on his lap. My father's friends did that, so I understood. I sat sideways and I put an arm around his shoulders and laughed at his jokes without listening to them. I kissed him to quiet him. His eyes never smiled. He tightened his grip on my thigh when I tried to slide off his lap, so I stayed.

When the infirmary said there was nothing else they could do for my aunt, I took her back to our room. She no longer needed shoes and socks, and in that way, there seemed to be more to spend. She had me buy electricity. "Let's watch those boys and girls," she said.

The boy who looked like the cook cheated at school. The girl who was secretly a woman loved a man, and he asked her to move into his home. She agreed.

When Dylan was on the screen, we watched and listened.

"That girl did well," my aunt nodded at the screen. "There's more to protection than moods."

—w—

There's no meat sometimes, but there's still seasoning. I traded one of my batteries for a little bottle of flakes where the label is partly picked off, but I can still make out MONTREAL GRILL. When it's my turn to cook whatever is brought back, I shake it on. Squirrels, gulls, dandelion greens. The old people who ate at my tables asked to speak to me. They told me it tastes like Friday nights a long time ago. The cook sent me back to the kitchen before they could say anything else, and he slapped me in the doorway because I took too long with them.

I wonder what Montreal is like. I know there is a big mountain and people speak French and the weather is more distant than it is here. I slip away from the kitchen while the cook is arguing with the dishwashers. I climb up to the roof. I figure out where the northeast is, where Montreal is. I sit facing that way, with my own city and the setting sun at my back. It's sprinkling a little. I pull up my hood. It gives me a place to whisper to Dylan how much I miss him. For centuries, everyone wore head coverings outdoors. Then for a little while, no one did. Now everyone does again. Hats. Boots. Cloaks. Weapons. Protection.

THE MYTH OF THE MOTHER AND CHILD

Michelle S. Lee

Foreword

Thus a heaviness thickened her
limbs. Her feet, so swift
in flight a moment ago, sank
to the earth and reeded
the riverbank, skin solidifying
into bark, hair hardening
into branch, hands splaying
into leaf. Her bones settled
against wind and stayed.

She'd fled not from men who claimed
to be gods, but a child who claimed
her uterus once and ate her
way out. But the feasting didn't
stop just then. The girl came back
for the heart.

Volume I

Before she bled, she believed
she would be an oracle, a conduit
from the voices chanting
through her to limbs and beating
heart, but then

he chased her so hard
she bruised her
psyche and could no longer
channel the pleas and demand
to worship something larger
than herself. He caught her
round the neck, round the breast
round the thigh and called
to the bleeding. *I am a god*, he said
and she lay with him willingly.

Volume II

When your hand rests on your round
belly and cups
a determined heel, you become an animal
filling with milk
and cry for a love that will never be
returned the way you want.

In the dark, the child always turns
to the father, even
when you sing until your voice dies
slowly and you dig a home in your side
with a spoon.

Volume III

She didn't need the arrow to fall
hard to her knees when the girl
was born.

Two hundred and seventy odd days
had passed of collapse
and eruption,

of impasse

and finally, a yielding.
Yes, she had fallen
long before

the girl burst
from her womb and tore
her heart

into pieces that she neatly
buttered and fit perfectly inside
her mouth.

Volume IV

She was cleaned on her mother's kitchen table
in a bowl of warmed water alongside the lamb
shanks and quinoa. The broth was as bloody
as the naming, which stirred the air with oaths
to that grandmother and this auntie and the dead
cousin thrice-removed but still beloved—until
she decided to name herself and spoke, leaving
all silenced and hands on knives.

Volume V

Beware: a child's look can grab
your gut like bread and leave you

grasping for crumbs.
You should expect it

in the moment after waking.
The child squeezes the yeast

and smells you up close
then opens her eyes and wants

the meat of you, sucks
past the sinew until only the marrow

is left for soup.

Volume VI

There are always stories about crones
who live in the woods and eat small
children—but what if
the stories are wrong?
What if the crones were being eaten
by small children bit by bit
over the years, so slowly
that the crones don't know
that once they were young
and their young skin has buckled
into frog-colored folds, don't know

that they once laid on grassy knolls
with sheepsmen disguised as gods
and counted the stars behind
youth and muscle, don't
know that the milk that once
filled their juicy breasts
has been suckled dry.
The small children keep this
to themselves and lure
the women with the scent
of newborn skin and cooing.
The small children laugh
because they are truly
the ones with the wisdom.

Volume VII

The crones didn't tell her
that she would fall in and out
of love—with the beat of her
heart and the blink of her
daughter's eyes—and slowly.

Volume VIII

In a house dug out of earth
in a corner warm with dung
a mother raised a girl. From
the time the girl was small
her mother whispered daily
about the power of hair.
Do not cut it, said her mother.

Do not bind it.
Do not wind it in braids.
The girl scoffed at the old wives'
tale that never seemed to end
but after she grew, the girl did not
cut her hair. Instead, she used it
to climb down from the cradle
of her mother's arms and wove
it into a sail which blew her
to places she believed held knowing
beyond her mother's, embraces
she believed held truths beyond
the umbilical. The mother prayed
the girl would never return.

Volume IX

Thus you are past your years of birthing
of lying in meadows with youth
of being chased by dogs wanting to keep
the smell of you on their bared teeth
of desperately needing to leave
the underworld because spring is coming
and you want to open yourself
like some bulb, greedily drinking
rain through the slit in your husk—

now you lie emptied of them
him
her
heart gone
root rot
no lining left

she looks you in the eyes
your daughter
the one who has been
inside you since you were born

the egg of her breaks
when she realizes you
were nothing but an egg
yourself once
inside another
woman
this story hers
passed along on fine bone
china and served warm
next to blood pudding.

SCHRÖDINGER'S WIFE

Robert Neilson

No David today.

No. He thought it would be better if I came by myself.

So it's about Joy.

Are we that predictable?

Afraid so.

Tell me what happened.

David was away on business.

Would you like a cup of tea?

Thanks.

I'll stick on the kettle. Go on.

I was bored. Maybe a little down. I've never really got used to him being away overnight. This time it was three days. I decided to redecorate Joy's bedroom.

Was there a specific reason?

I just wanted something more appropriate to a seven-year-old. So I took the opportunity to make a mess while he was away. I cleared out the baby stuff and stripped the walls, went and picked new wallpaper. I was really pleased with it: a floral print. And I got some great furniture from a little place in Dalkey. Goode Homes, with an *e*, I think it's called.

Goode Rooms.

You know it, Simon?

My wife likes to shop.

It's a bit expensive, but money is one thing David never complains about. Anyway, I hung the wallpaper myself—it wasn't as hard as I'd been led to believe—and had everything ready for the furniture delivery. I was sweeping up the last of the dust and shreds of old paper when he arrived back. I honestly thought he'd be pleased. But he threw a bit of a knicker fit. Started shouting.

Because you didn't consult him?

He said afterwards that it was because he was worried about me. "I thought you were over all that," he said. Over it, Simon? He knows I'll never be over it. I thought he had accepted that I cope in whatever way I can.

We only discuss Joy at sessions David doesn't come to.

We never discuss Joy at home either. Except . . .

Except?

Except when I do something to force the issue.

Is that why you redecorated?

No. I told you, I wanted the room decorated for a little girl her age.

Nothing else?

I thought you, of all people, would understand, Simon.

I just need to be sure that we're on the same page, Karen. Two sugars?

Thanks. Are you worried that I'm going psycho? David is. A bit, I think.

Maybe you should reassure him.

I did.

What did you tell him?

I told him that I was fully aware that Joy died when she was one day old. I told him that I was aware that I had built up this fantasy of her. I didn't think she actually wore the clothes in the wardrobe or played with the toys. I told him that buying them helped keep me sane. That pretending she existed helped sometimes. That talking to her once in a while helped get me through tough times. That sometimes I was still going to cry myself to sleep no matter how hard I pretended. But it's a game I need to play, and you, Simon, said it was harmless as long as I didn't confuse it with reality. Stayed grounded, I think you said.

And you think redecorating her room is appropriate?

We have the money. There's just the two of us. Always will be.

I wish David would talk about Joy in these sessions. It would be healthy to get it out into the open.

I was surprised he agreed to come to couples counseling. He still looks on it as counseling for me. He doesn't need it.

You think he does?

She was his daughter too, Simon. He wanted children as much as I did. He just keeps it all bottled up better than me.

I'm convinced we'll get him talking about it one of these days.

Don't hold your breath.

—ᗰ—

No need to ask why he didn't come this time.

No.

Was there a fight?

Sometimes I wish it was like that. But we never fight about her anymore. He just seems so sad whenever the subject of Joy comes up. I don't think I could actually fight with him.

What was it this time?

I keep a box in the attic. It's got Joy's special things in it.

What sort of things?

Her first shoes. A dress from when she was a year old. A photo of Elmer; she really loved that dog. A copy of *Town Mouse and Country Mouse*. I read that to her over and over. The Live Aid single. And that song by The Cars that was featured in the video they showed during the concert. I can't hear it without crying, still. A nightshirt I made for her with Little Miss Scatterbrain on it. She loved that. It was just a big tee shirt that I drew the Little Miss on. The *Sunday Times* special on Princess Diana and Elton John's single. A couple of dolls. Her favorite teddy. The 1988 Jackie Annual. Just stuff.

David didn't know you were keeping them?

I guess not. I was sitting on the edge of the trapdoor into the attic, leaning my feet on the second rung from the top, flicking through the Town Mouse and Country Mouse. I was putting her Sweet Sixteen birthday card into it when I started to browse. He came looking for me. He was going to cook dinner and wondered if I fancied a nice piece of haddock. Then he asked, "What are you doing up there?" And I said he should come and see. I pulled up my legs to make room for him and he climbed the ladder, head and shoulders sticking into the attic. I showed him the book, then the other things. He took hold of my hand and said, "I wish you wouldn't do this to yourself, Karen." Then he began to cry. I tried to comfort him, but given that he was only half up the attic ladder and I was kneeling over him, it just didn't work. He went back down to the kitchen and began to cook. By the time I got Joy's box stowed away, David wanted to treat it as if nothing happened.

Did he ask you to come and speak to me about it?

No. He just said this morning that he wouldn't be coming. He thought we might have things to discuss without him.

Which means Joy.

Is there any other reason to worry about my sanity?

Only one.

Oh?

You still call me Simon.

You said you didn't mind. I don't know why David thought it was your name. You should have corrected him at once instead of letting us go on using the wrong name for . . . what? Five or six sessions.

Did you ever tell him?

He would never have come back. He can be terribly pompous and self-important. I can still hear him introducing us.

Surely you could tell him now.

Probably. But it's not worth the risk. He might just get it into his head that we laugh about it behind his back in the sessions he doesn't come to. That it's our little secret. I mean, we've been coming here for a dozen years and I still think he'd stop at the smallest excuse. You've got to remember, I'm the nutty one.

It's hard to forget.

Oh, you!

He's really that insecure about counseling?

He really is. Counseling isn't for normal people like us. It's for Americans and alcoholics and the like, as far as he's concerned.

We'll drag him kicking and screaming into the twentieth century one of these days.

Possibly even while it's still the twentieth century.

Good to see you both. Would you mind if I made an observation, David?

Not at all.

You look happy. You usually look, if you don't mind my saying so, like you're here under duress.

I'm here to talk about Joy.

Wow! I never thought I'd hear you say those particular words. That's great. Why the change of heart?

Do you want to tell it, love?

No, David, I think Simon would prefer to hear it from you.

I suppose he deserves it after putting up with me for so long.

What is it, fifteen years?

Nineteen.

That long.

Do you have other clients who've been with you as long?

Not even close.

Karen had . . . we had a lot of issues. I guess you know I've never really bought into the whole therapy thing. But I wish we'd come to you sooner. Right after . . . Joy and the . . . and Karen's hysterectomy and . . . all that fucking coping. But that's what one was supposed to do. Cope. You didn't air your dirty washing in public. You kept it to yourself. Got on with it. Dealt with it as best you could, then moved on. That's what my parents did, and what I expected to do. And I apologize for my attitude over the years. I don't know if we'd have made it without you. But I think we have made it. We had our twenty-fifth anniversary last week. And the next twenty-five are going to be great.

You both look, I guess, happier that I've ever seen you.

We are. And it's my fault. Or at least it was my fault that we weren't as happy as we could be. I knew Karen needed Joy, but I couldn't accept that there was room for her in my life. I thought it was Karen's problem, not our problem.

That's fantastic, David. But I have to ask, did something happen to trigger all this?

I suppose. In a way, I've grown used to the bedroom decorations changing every few years. It really pissed me off the first time but I kind of realized it made Karen happy, so it was for the best. So three or four weeks ago, a couple of days after our last session, I came home and she was up in Joy's room. I wondered what it would be this time. I steeled myself for it and headed upstairs. The room was empty. All the posters were down off the wall and the teenager's bedroom had disappeared, bed, wardrobe and all. Naturally, I was curious about what was going in there in its place. Karen says, "I was thinking I might turn it into a sewing room now that she's moved out." Then she looked at me and smiled. "Don't be so surprised. You didn't think she was going to stay with us forever did you? She's got to spread her wings, live her own life, get her own place. Time to move on."

Just like that?

Yes, just like that. I realized that there was nothing wrong with Karen's fantasies about a daughter. But I didn't realize it until she was gone.

Will she be visiting?

If she does, we have a guest room.

Of course. And will you, Karen . . . is she . . .

I do believe, Simon, you're trying to ask me if I'll still have a relationship with Joy now that she's moved out. What sort of a mother would I be to abandon her now?

And I'm accepting that I'm her father and am looking forward to hearing about her life, even if it is at second hand. Karen told me she has a boyfriend.

They're thinking about moving in together. Karen's flat is big enough for them to share for a while.

I never saw this coming, I have to admit.

It couldn't have happened without you, Simon. We're really grateful to you. Both of us. Aren't we David?

Absolutely. And don't think it's the last you'll see of us. I'm still crackers.

David!

The term we prefer is bat-shit crazy.

I wish Simon was here.

Simon?

Your colleague. Paul. We, my husband and I, thought his name was Simon when we first came to him. It's a long story. I didn't know he was sick. How is he doing?

He's okay, but he won't be back in harness for at least a couple of months.

Can you help, jumping into the middle of my problems like this?

Your summary of the past thirty some years was concise and comprehensive. I think I understand the situation. But you're going to have to go over today's events again, maybe a little more slowly. I'm not sure I caught it all.

I'm sorry—Mark, is that right? I was a bit frazzled when I came in.

You're calm now. We can go over it all again in detail. How's your tea, by the way?

Lovely, thanks. Just the way I like it. I'm not really allowed tea these days. My doctor says it's bad for my angina. But in troubled times there's nothing quite like a nice cup of tea to put things right.

Perhaps you could start again from the beginning.

Yes. Right. Let me see . . . I was standing outside the supermarket waiting for my taxi. Usually David picks me up, but he is visiting his sister in Hull. She's not well. At our age, it seems that everyone we know is dead or dying or sick . . . Sorry. Where was I? Oh yes, outside the supermarket. And there were two lovely little girls standing nearby. I noticed them particularly because they looked to be exactly the ages of my grandchildren.

I'd rather not beat around the bush, so I'll be frank in my questions.

Of course.

I just need to check. These would be your fantasy grandchildren?

Yes. Joy's daughters. They're ten and nine.

These girls reminded you of them?

Yes. And I thought if I had a photograph of these little girls it would be exactly like having a photo of Joy's daughters.

You recognized them?

No. I've never really been able to conjure their faces. In my mind they're, if you like, generic nine- and ten-year-olds. But I would have liked these girls to be my granddaughters. They looked like lovely children, so well behaved, standing there quietly, waiting.

And they spoke to you.

Yes. I told you that. One of them walked up to me, the older one. Her little sister followed but stood a little behind. The older one said, "You look just like our granny." I didn't really know what to say to her. I tried to give her a reassuring smile. "We have a picture," the younger one said, "a picture of you." The older one turned and shushed her. I told her that if I had grandchildren, I would want them to be exactly like her and her sister. "Why don't you love us?" the little one asked. The older child turned to her sister and said, "I warned you not to start." I told them that I wished I was their granny. "You never liked our dad, did you? That's why you never came to see us," said the younger one. She was treating me as though I actually was her grandmother. I understood then that some awful family tragedy was being acted out before my eyes. I felt I could help because . . . because of Joy, I suppose. So I asked if their mother was with them. The little one hissed at me, "How could you." Her sister said, "Our dad will be here in a minute." That was a relief. The younger child was getting quite upset. She said, "You don't care about us and you never cared about our mum." I didn't know how to respond. She seemed so certain. There was no doubt in her mind that I was her grandmother, as far as I could tell. The older one never corrected her sister's impression; she seemed to accept it totally. Her only concern was that her sister had come out with it right up front.

Were you at all worried that they might . . . I don't know, get violent or something? Start screaming?

Yes, a little. I looked around, but no one else seemed to have noticed anything amiss about our conversation. Then the little one began to cry. "I hate you," she said. Her sister pulled her into an embrace. Patted her back. Said, "There, there, you'll be all right. Don't upset yourself over *her*." And some other stuff I didn't really hear. A man was approaching; I assumed it was the father. He said, "Proud of yourself, Karen?"

He knew your name?

I think that's what he said. It's a bit fuzzy right now. But I think he called me by my name.

Go on.

"Proud of yourself?" he said. I just looked at him, probably with my mouth open. I was flabbergasted. This total stranger and his children had mistaken me for someone else. I tried to explain this to him. He said, "You're a cold fish, abandoning your daughter like that. Didn't come to the wedding. Never came to the hospital to see your grandchildren when they were born. Didn't even come to Joy's funeral." I said, "Joy?" It came out as a whisper. "Your daughter. My wife. Their mother. Joy. She pointed you out on the street for us. You just breezed past, oblivious. It's not like your life was so full you'd no room for us. You never did remarry, did you?" My Joy? I looked into those little faces staring up at me. I could see something like hate in the set of the little one's mouth. But there was something else in her eyes. In her sister's as well. Something like hope. Something that could so easily be love. The father took his daughters by the hand and pulled them away from me. "How could you?" he said again. "Why punish children, for—" He stopped, coughing a bitter laugh. "I don't even know why you cut yourself off from Joy. What could she have done? She never said a bad word about you. You were her mum and she loved you. So much." Then he repeated, "So much," and walked away.

Does it feel better, talking about it?

A bit, I suppose.

I hate to say this, Karen, but I have a client due in a minute or two. We're going to have to wrap up.

Of course. Thanks for fitting me in at such short notice.

I hope it helped.

I . . . Yes.

Karen, are you okay? My receptionist is a bit worried about you.

I'll be fine in a minute. I just needed to sit for a while.

You've been crying. I don't think you're fine at all. Is there someone I can call to come and get you? Take you home.

Nobody. David's in Hull.

Maybe—

I hope.

You hope? What is it you hope?

I'm afraid.

Afraid of what? That man? Did he threaten you?

No. Not at all. It's not that. I'm afraid . . .

Yes?

Maybe I'm losing my mind. I mean, I've been in therapy for thirty years. Maybe I've always been . . . bat-shit-crazy is, I believe, the correct medical term.

Why do you think that?

This man, these children, they seemed so sure that they knew me, that they knew Joy.

But Joy only exists in your head.

What if she didn't?

I don't think I'm following you.

What if the man and his children are right? I am his mother-in-law, their granny.

I don't think that's a healthy line to follow.

But what if it's true? What then?

You know that it's not true.

Do I? How can I be sure?

I'm going to order a taxi to take you home. If you still feel anxious tomorrow, call me and I'll fit you in.

I don't want to go home. I'm afraid.

What do you have to be afraid of?

If they are right, then the world I've been living in is a tragic lie. If they're wrong, I lose my grandchildren.

But there's no tragedy if they're right. You did have a daughter. You had her for a long time.

He said I never remarried.

I didn't know you'd been married before David.

I wasn't. David's my one and only.

I'm afraid I'm being a little slow.

You know about Schrödinger's Cat?

Sure, it's both dead and alive until you open the box.

And until I go home I have both a husband and two beautiful grand-children.

I— I don't know . . .

Neither do I.

BLUENESS

Libby Hart

Erase an astronaut's view of the earth.
Erase the color of his eyes.
Erase midnight. Erase cobalt.
Erase sapphire, navy, and cyan.

Erase the black dog. Erase blue heelers.
Erase blue moons, blueprints, and blue movies.

Erase the bruise. Erase the blue-rinse.
Erase bluestockings, blue-collars, and bluejackets.

Erase the scream. Erase blue funk.
Erase Bluebeard, blue-bellied black snakes, and Blue Devil.

Erase the mistakes. Erase the bluebloods.
Erase blue ribbons, blue chips, and blue cheese.

Erase the waves. Erase blue swimmers.
Erase bluebottles, blue-ringed octopuses, and blue sharks.

Erase the thrush's egg. Erase the blue wren.
Erase bluetits, blue cranes, and bluebirds.

Erase the argument.
Erase the blues.
Erase bluegrass.
Erase the bluer, bluest blue.

LOVE IN VAIN

John Newman

Maisy saw him first, so she ran inside to tell her momma. Althea was making a tart bramble pie.

"What man?" she said.

"I don't know, Momma. He's all dressed in black and carryin' somethin'. And he's walkin' here and his feet don't make no dust at all."

Althea wiped her hands down and told Maisy to go in back and wait there. Then she stepped outside.

"Robert Johnson," she said. The man rested his guitar case.

"Hello, Althea."

Althea looked around.

"You better come on in my kitchen." Robert stepped up and past her and inside her house.

Althea poured a glass of water from the covered jug, handed it to Robert. He set it down on the table.

"That some nice suit, Robert," she said.

"White fella from New York City bought me this. Wants to take me to New York, play in a concert hall."

Althea backed away, leaned against the wall.

"Guess you famous."

Robert looked straight back at her.

"Don't believe I'm ever gonna see New York City, Althea," he said. "Don't believe I will." He looked around. "Asked about you in town. Said you took up with Web Kinsella. This Web's house?"

Althea nodded. Robert ran one long finger down the side of the glass; Althea watched as a bubble appeared. He took his finger away, and the bubble disappeared.

"He wouldn't like to know you was here, Robert."

Robert took off his hat, spun it around his finger, dropped it on the table.

"I don't know nothin' bout Web 'cept what I heard." He smiled, slightly. "Don't feel it does a man justice to go on what folks says about him."

"Maisy, don't touch that guitar!" Althea bolted into the other room and tore the child's hand away before she could unlatch the case. And then Robert was at her shoulder.

"Don't harm her jus' to look," he whispered. But that made Althea mad. Made her frightened too, and she slapped Maisy's ass and told her go play outside. Maisy started sobbing, but another slap got her moving anyway.

Robert watched as the child scampered away.

"You figurin', Robert?" There was a hard edge to Althea now; now that the business might be coming out. Robert lit a cigarette with a fancy lighter and blew out a stream of smoke.

"She ain't yours," Althea said it right up close. Robert just shrugged.

"If you say so."

"What you doin' here, Mister Johnson?" Althea closed the front door. Then she buttoned up her house dress before she turned back inside.

"Playin' Harlan's jook, over in Greensville. After midnight, 'course." Robert was comfortable now, set back on the chair, in the shadows. Althea felt herself draw closer, felt some sort of sweat breaking out inside her, and then a breeze blew past, cooling, lifting aside the blanket to the bedroom. Robert smiled.

"What you doin' here?" she said it again. Robert reached inside his jacket and pulled out a photograph.

"Remember that?"

Althea took the photograph and almost laughed in spite of it all.

"Oh, look at you, Robert." She traced a finger around the image: a ridiculous manboy, his grin splitting up half his fool head, clutching a guitar, leaning forward into the camera like as if he couldn't wait for something.

She turned the picture over and looked at the faded stamp.

"Roosevelt Studio, Jackson," she murmured.

"You remember that, Althea?" he asked again, and she set down next to him.

"'Course I do," she smiled. She held the picture up in front and looked back and forth to the man beside her.

"You ain't shook hands with this man in a long time, Robert." Her voice was sad. She held the photograph out, but he stood up and buttoned his coat.

"You keep it," he said. He walked to the door, turned. "Maybe I can stop in again, say hello to Web?" and then he was gone.

When the sun started going down Althea was in the kitchen again, listening for Web's footsteps. Listening for how he threw open the door to tell her if he was drinking.

She knew he'd be drinking today. Knew he'd be drinking a lot.

Sometimes, when he had a lot of liquor, Web beat her for a witch. Their talking never got directly around to Robert Johnson, but when he beat her that's what he beat her for. Mostly he didn't have enough liquor or enough money for that type of drinking, and then he was careful, suspicious.

"You purposely shamin' me, woman?" He was behind her now, and she never even heard him come in. Web's face was purple and his fists kept to clenching up.

"They sayin' all about how Robert Johnson come lookin' for you. How he come into my house!"

Althea stood back. She wasn't scared, just puzzled. Web's eyes kept flinching around as though to find a trace of Robert in the walls or on the ceiling.

"You ain't drunk, Web?"

He ripped from the kitchen and pushed Maisy outside. Before he come back in he slapped the wall hard.

"Got no damn money, woman," he yelped. "Got me no damn woman 'cept a witch, and I got me no damn money for drinkin'!"

Althea scraped out the skillet on Web's plate and set it down on the table.

"You know what I hate the most is when you punch me in the nose, Web." She didn't know where these words were coming from, and all she could feel was what she might look like if Web beat her to death that night.

"Blood goes all over, and I can't never get it out. Scares Maisy too, thinks I'm dyin'." She looked straight to him, "You ain't gonna do that again."

"He lay with you?"

Althea shook her head. This time Web screamed, grabbed her arms and took hold of her collar like he might tear her away naked.

"He lay with you, Althea? You sweat him up in my bed?" and he hurled her across the kitchen. She couldn't stop her head from hitting first, and when she woke up it was dark.

What she heard was a scrape of shoes and a clink of glass, and then voices . . . maybe just one voice. She heard Robert Johnson as he unlatched his guitar case and sat down on the hard back wooden chair out in the big room.

She pulled herself up and slipped along the wall to the doorway. There was that clink again. Web had a bottle of whisky. Robert sat opposite, plucked at a string or two and fiddled with his guitar. He wasn't even looking close to her when he said, "You want me to play for you, Althea?"

She stepped into the room, Web never looked up, he just seemed all frozen, couldn't take his eyes away from Robert.

"You want me to play something, Web?" and Web said nothing. Robert's thumb hit the top string, started dancing along like an eel, and his foot tapped up and down. And then the sounds came, the sounds Althea been hearing about, sounds everybody been whispering about. She stared at his fingers, wondering how he made that guitar cry and moan and play like there might have been three men playing at once.

Althea let herself slip down the wall to the floor, wrapped herself in that song until it was over, and then the silence was strange.

Web's voice trembled. "People say you went down to the crossroads, Robert."

Robert just put away his guitar.

Althea laughed. "You never played like that in Jackson." She smiled. "You remember how you wanted to play with Son House and Charlie Patton? And they wouldn't let you."

Web's head spun around when she spoke but he didn't say nothing. Althea looked at her man and smiled again.

"You go down to the crossroads, Robert? You find someone who could tune your guitar?"

Robert pulled up the bottle and raised it to his lips. The liquor slid down smooth before he spoke.

"Ain't no need to talk about such things, Althea. Ain't no thing to talk about."

"What you come for Robert? Come for my Althea?"

Robert snapped shut the latches on his case and stood up. "Maybe I did, Web." He handed Web the bottle.

"You want to come out with me tonight, Web?"

"Come out where?" Web was scared.

Robert picked up his case and walked to the door. "Come out and see me play, like Althea used to do. You got no money for drinkin', but I do."

Web looked all around, looked to Althea but her face was empty, and her eyes said nothing. He licked his lips. "And then what? What do we do after that, Robert?" Robert ran his hand down Althea's cheek. "After that we can talk."

Web got to his feet. "Got somethin' in the kitchen," he muttered. Robert half laughed. "Well go on," he said.

Robert reached out his hand and Althea touched it.

"Do somethin' for me, Althea?" he asked, and she laid his hand against her cheek. "If you want," she whispered.

"Look on that picture sometime, shine a light on me?"

Web come back in from the kitchen and stood watching. Althea rested back against the chair, let Robert Johnson slip away from her, didn't barely hear it when the two men stepped out into the darkness and were gone.

BETWEEN

xTx

I push the wall when he isn't looking or when he is asleep or when he's left the room. I step through. There is no hallway. No transition. Just an open door and a new room. The air between them both catching in each other's mouths.

If she's in the room when I step through she always looks to see what I'm leaving—I only let her know so much. Her head tilts right-left, right-left; her eyes trying to get around me. I close it as quick as I can. I go to her.

I spend minutes, hours, sometimes days. Time goes by the same on either side of the wall and it never seems to make a difference. I've tested. I've tried. I was cautious at first, only risking brief visits, spending only hesitant moments. I would shake my head shyly and stand just inside the closed wall, shifting my weight from one foot to the other, my back less than a foot from where I had come, while she patted the edge of the bed talking in a whisper, smiling. Every visit I came a little closer. Stayed a little longer. It was a process. It was a need. She never gave up on me. Still hasn't. Won't.

He doesn't ask where I go. I'm not sure if he even knows I am gone. I want to feel that my absence leaves some sort of void, something that could be missed. But whenever I come back from her, he never looks up, never looks away from the television. Even when the wall closes loudly. Even when I slam it. "What's for dinner?" "Did you make my appointment?" "Can you hand me the remote?" Always questions like that. Never the questions I wait to hear. I've stopped waiting. I could wait until I die, I think.

She never talks about things unless I want to talk about them. She knows there is so much I need to hide. Things like her, but that is different. She treats the things I don't say the same way she treated my initial visits; whispers, smiles, pats of bed. I inch forward, the speed of a span of many years.

I walk the familiar pathways of the home I share with him, imagining the scars on our carpet, how I should see them; bare and pressed from so much of the same walking. But there is nothing. No evidence. How can a surface so used look so much the same? I wonder about my skin, my soul, and how much something can take before it breaks.

Her voice is sweet confidence and I can never wait to hear it. Sometimes, when the light outside settles to a gray blue and he is somewhere not caring, I put my ear to the wall but there is always silence. So I push the wall, I go inside, I close the wall and ask her to tell me about her day and she always does. I revel in her world. The shine of what she does. So many important things with colleagues, family, friends and men who shower her with everything she deserves. Sometimes I lower my head, ashamed of what I can't give her but she always lifts it. It only takes two fingers.

I feel the light that she has put inside me fighting to get out. I will my pores closed. I close my eyes, press my nostrils shut but it burns so hot I am sure there must be a glow. I am scared he will see when the lights are off. He never does. Or never says anything. Or reads by the light of me when my eyes are closed.

I lie next to her in her big bed. She does things to me. Things she knows I like. Sometimes we do things to each other. Most of the time we just stay entwined, creating that third warmth that two bodies make when they stay so close together. She tells me, "I dream about you every night and in the dreams you always look so sad." Then she glances at the wall and I move her face back to where it's looking at me. Seeing me.

I leave her covered in lipstick; my throat, my mouth ripe with smears. When the wall closes behind me he doesn't turn or move. I wave my hand in front of his face. It brings nothing. I head for a mirror to make sure I am still there. I lick my fingers and press them into the smears. I put the smears into my mouth. I press again. They are not coming off. I wonder if he'd hear me if I screamed. I want to take his hand, lick his fingers, bring them to my face and press them, press them, press them . . .

I wait until she isn't looking or when she is asleep or when she's left the room before pushing on the wall. But she knows anyway. I see her droop a little or hear her sigh. My chest tightens, as it always does, but I push anyway. Her place is not where I belong, even though it is. We both know this. It is understood.

I come back in. As the wall shuts behind me he walks past. I know I smell of perfume, sex. I know my shirt hangs, unbuttoned and my hair is mussed, sweaty, but he barely acknowledges me. I light myself on fire. I wait.

TENNESSEE

Thia Li Colvin

My father was a pretty big guy, but now I got him in a jar in my closet.
He ain't so big now.

A DREAM OF THE AZTEC

Edmund Zagorin

Particles of sand cling to the boy's hands. He rubs his fingers together, knocking the red grains to the floor where they lie amongst the corn-rows of cheap blue airplane carpet. But then . . . then the boy wakes up (again) and the sand has returned, hooked onto the miniscule ridges of his fingertips. The boy cannot simply take off so easily without a residue of the desert hitchhiking along. It is the spring of '89. Pan Am Flight 103 has just crashed into a small town in Scotland called Lockerbie, and everyone talks about airplanes with confused whispers, nervous anger.

Ugh. Vaseline nausea and soft paraffin memories bubbling up. Sand and the scalding sun, and a shadow, always a shadow. Those metallic rays lacerate his shoulders; their brass thread sutures his mouth into submission and leaves his legs burnt-sugar brown. Volition has little to do with this half-reclined airplane seat, the recycled air in his lungs, his trajectory over the clouds to a strange city. The red sand takes its own path, leaving . . . a trace of that taut silhouette standing over him, masqued, beckoning. The boy's hands splay backwards into the warm folds of reddish dustcream. He squints up into the effervescence of desert twilight and a man's black hair. A shadow's flexion, practically written onto his chest by now.

The boy's name is Mero, only if anyone asks. A normal man sits in the airplane seat next to him, restless. He stretches his normal hands over his normal head and cracks his normal knuckles towards the egg-cartoned cabin ceiling that rattles with the motion of the engines. Mero's stomach throbs with Arturo's necessities. Shadows, chopped up into little fists of latex, dreading the prospect of unhappy rebirth. The normal man's a modern cowboy, ruddy-faced, with the throat clearing habit of a lifelong smoker and a big gold-colored class ring on his powerful left hand. Mero notes all this without breaking a hard double-squint. The normal man is also white-skinned, or at least had been before his trip to the Southern desert; a cowboy, not a *gaucho*. Suspicious, this man. Vigilant. The type who doesn't share armrests without a fight. Mero can also tell that the cowboy wants to beat the shit out of him but otherwise is doing his best to pretend that Mero doesn't exist.

Fine by me. Mero folds his slender arms down into his lap, wrists barely touching. Veins crawl up just under the skin of his inner wrist, quivering beneath a hollow star tattoo. He looks down again at his fingers, at the grains of fine red sand stuck to the sweat-damp flesh; a granulated glove. Shake and shake again. Is it gone yet? Mero's hands feel guiltily warm; a fresh crime scene.

The stewardess gives Mero a ginger ale. She has this plastic name tag with silver-foil wings pointing out on either side: ANNALIS. Her wilted smile asks for silence, and Mero gives all he has. I know why shutting up and thrusting a tight-lipped smile onto my wind-burned *mestizo* face might be the best thing that happens to you all day. Which reminds him that Annalis, the cowboy, and everyone else is probably terrified of him. I guess they think I'm the Devil. Maybe they saw my horns. This time he smiles for real. Mero can put on a pretty good grin when he wants.

Air travel may produce a disorienting sensation, separating the *orbis* of mind and body, a mis-alignment of here and now, place and moment. Each second this Boeing 757 moves Mero further and further away from the familiar, towards . . . An awakening, from dreams dragged backwards through the Boeing's chem trails to a desert, dreams now dashing to keep up as the aircraft traverses horizon after horizon. It's even more discombobulating when the itinerant flightline crosses the equator, charting a course through too many sun-drenched fantasies and a stomach full of powdered destiny (just add water, stir carefully).

The little girl a row forward and across from him grabs at her seatbelt buckle in sleep, twisting it. It's all part of the choreography, the set dressing. Tessellated patterns on the seatback. Small foil-wrapped astro-sacs of peanuts. Nurse-white barf bags neatly folded in the seat back. The two jowly American ranchers in front of Mero trading jocular vacation stories. The snoozing cowboy next to him, his features inlaid with the exscription of high-altitude iridescence. Mero sighs drowsily.

Never before has Mero left his hometown, his country. Now he's riding high, taking his bird-of-paradise body all the way to New York City, and on Arturo's dime to boot! He wrinkles his bell pepper nose, pushes its tip inward like a button to massage the cartilage. Mero flicks the brass piercing on the back of his neck, shaped like a zipper-tab, concealed by dirty knots of dark brown hair with patchy orange highlights. It gets cold sometimes, the stud. He wears a sleeveless shirt of orange mesh, tight-fitting and diaphanous, through which inquiring eyes can espy the hard purple embossments of his nipples. The cowboy crosses his unsleeping legs away from Mero, concealing an irate tumescence. Mero smiles viciously, galvanized with stolen radiance. In other words, he looks like an Angel.

Suddenly, the airplane jolts. The collective reverie bursts open, milkweedy and twitching. The cabin's stillness left lying in shards on the cheap blue carpet. Tremors shake hard, rattling bodies; eyes open, heads look around. The jolt comes clattering again, harder this time. Whispers of concern. From the airplane's subterranean recesses, an unseen baby begins bawling. The seats wobble. Beneath the pallid jaws of grim-faced men, sweatered golf torsos take a stand. "What's going on? Do something!" But there is nothing to be done. The aisle is a twanging diving board, tilting out into . . . (don't look down) . . . and below? Mero gulps, swallowing a diamond. The sweaters sit back down hard as the plane thuds heavily against another implacable dune of wind.

They've entered an atmospheric wilderness, angry and pummeling. No mercy from sand, no mercy from vapors. The clouds slap the aircraft's aluminum with a dull thwack, as if they really have discovered a Firmament. Mero's mind fills with syrupy dread. All sorts of useless instincts stir from their slumbers, artlessly mobilized by shots of survival adrenaline. The cabin smells sour with the odor of sudden sweat, of bodies come alive with fear and trembling against the unseen terror.

Mero suddenly feels every grain of sand clinging to his skin. He urgently needs to clean himself. *Con permiso*. Hands begin rubbing at his body's corners as if animated with a life of their own, rubbing at the places where the burning sand grips his new sweat. That red sand, the sand of Arturo. His hands like nervous servants are preparing him for death. The cowboy gives him the dirtiest of looks. "Hey kid, willya sit still a sec?" The man is furious to be awake, to be aware; everyone is furious. Mero's mouth opens in terror, his breathing quickening. He must be clean of this infernal sand! The hot whisper of Arturo behind his ear . . .

Arturo's wild head digging at the hollow in Mero's collarbone. The air crushed out of Mero's adolescent chest, breathless with ecstasy. His buried eyes catch the light out beyond the railing of their decadent faux-Castilian balcony. Thin intervals of forgetting. A withered palm frond hangs down into Mero's immaculate gaze, a trompe l'oeil on the distant sunset. His vanishing point punctured with Arturo's primordial rhythm. They are so far in that room, so lost deep inside one another. Arturo's gnawed lips on the back of Mero's neck, his black tongue gripping the boy's piercing, lapping up the sweat and crust of desert sand. And . . .

There's a soft *ding* and the FASTEN SEATBELT light comes on. The captain makes a garbled announcement. "Mngamvera . . . zr . . . panic . . . fine . . . turbulence."

How accustomed, Mero thinks, how perfectly acclimated we all are to being reassured by an anonymous voice, a disembodied voice that has never before had the opportunity to lose our trust. And yet, no one in the cabin seems particularly comforted, as the airplane hits another speed-bump and careens into more empty air. It makes Mero wonder if they have been snared by some ethereal Fisherman casting His line down into the blue-pooled sky, awaiting foolish humans for prey or sport. Such a flimsy craft, thinks Mero, that its boasts cannot answer even the winds, that it shudders and bucks amongst the whorls of vapor, utterly helpless.

The passengers metastasize a collective uneasiness, malignant and uncontrollable. Whispers relay race up and down the cabin like shivers tracing a spine. Mothers "shhh, shhh" rubbing their children's backs, wiping away tears that stream down the small ones' red-crinkled faces. The sweatered men, the vacationers, the industrialists are at a loss. Mero sees one pretending to calmly read the Wall Street Journal. A black-haired

Spaniard clasps his hands in prayer, and Mero notes with disgust the tremble on his lips.

The line of old men waiting for the bathroom capsizes once, then twice, and only now do they realize that their bladders must submit to the imminent danger. These men have the faces of survivors, surviving. Together they grasp one another's cardigan elbows, and smile liplessly, "It's just like in the war, eh Herman?" And now they are thrown, first against the cabin wall and then into a row of Japanese schoolgirls, who look entirely nonplussed, amused and then deeply ashamed. The aircraft hull's shuddering calms down for only a moment and the old men hurry back to their seats, poisonously thwarted. They sit with annoyed resolve, crossing their legs.

Mero considers fainting. If only aircraft really could traverse backwards across time! The dirigibles of his memory float in reverse, circling the red desert of Arturo's body, peering down onto the landscape of a face that has been worn for twenty lifetimes of indifference. He notes the cacti of stiff black hair that have grown up around the rich oasis of a mouth. It is a snarling oasis, spitting curses as its owner lies in an uneasy slumber.

Then the shaking returns with unrestrained intensity. The aircraft bounces off a string of unyielding moguls (thwap-thwap-thwap!) that threaten to split the cabin stem to stern. This turbulence has that flavor of zero hour. The bottom goes out of everyone's stomach. The airplane plunges into the void. Another garbled announcement over the cabin speakers, this one even less reassuring in timbre. Mero's very vision is thrumming. The patterned blue seatbacks blur into a blistering fury. This time it's not a single sharp blow. Everything begins shaking, softly at first and then much harder. The outline of every object, of every person suddenly becomes indistinct, perhaps preparing for an ontological merger at the molecular level. From the back a baby's shriek oscillates and gathers momentum. This kid's really going for broke, Mero thinks; the scream to end all babyscreams. It crescendos in a throbbing bundle of infantile confusion, wrenching through the cabin in a Category 6 howl. Where is all that soft white noise when you need it?

The shaking chatters Mero's teeth without any effort on the part of his jaw. Bile rises unbidden along with an occluded sense-memory . . . The copper taste of hard-boiled darkness. The patina of Arturo's dilating caress. If only those wax-winged capsules can fend off my gastric fury, flying up here so close to the sun. Will they find those little crimes ripped from my torso, melted rubber and white sin amidst the wreckage? Or will everything simply catch flames?

A prayer Mero once heard crawls back to him from the mouth of some grandmotherly ancestor. A drawn mouth, papery with wind scars, carefully intoning, slowly stacking word on word in her tiny old language. Mero's face hard, stiff against the shock waves, thick with capillaries of black blood. WHAMWHAMWHAMWHAMWHAMWHAM. The Boeing shakes. It's losing the boxing match.

Across the aisle from Mero an old foreigner's eyes are closed and his knuckles grow white at the tapered ends of his armrests. His long hands curving down, gripping. He's rail-thin, with straight grey hair, and appears to be the kind of man who may once have played the oboe. Mero tries counting backwards, but his body cannot stop quivering.

"Kid, how bout sitting still for a sec . . . Cut it out, ya hear?" The cowboy is agitated, the sound of a threat in his voice. The cowboy's beady gaze is laced with hatequeer loathing.

Mero tries to restrain his convulsing body, but it is like trying to hold a handful of writhing eels that keep slipping away. Both he and the cowboy have erections.

All around him the desperate murmurs of the other passengers multiply, growing louder and louder. Engorged on terror. They glance at him, tight-lipped, at the orange mesh of his shirt, at his soft brown face. They know what he is. Wearing that—it is no way to die; he'll make a shameful corpse. Buttery sweat glazes the passengers with primal hormones, the dull ache of unsatisfied bloodlust. Mero knows they suspect him, the reprobate; the intended target of this dizzying revenge. "Throw the queer off, save the children!" barks the voice of Mero's practiced self-immolation fantasy, hoarse and feverish. It hangs from each grain of sand like ballast from the hot air balloon of his body, marking him as that fatal weight that must be ejected for uncontaminated passengers to survive.

Mero's panic is white-hot, a point that sticks in his chest, filling his nostrils with metallic fumes. The engines scream; they're going down. He buries his mind in whatever scraps of frizzy noise he can gather, covers everything with their chaotic patterns of humming and rushing. Forming a substance out of their emptiness. He tries concentrating, first on abstractions and then on concrete images: a sunflower absolutely motionless in a blue glass vase, a metal pot full of boiled beans, the absent smile of the famous footballer Claudio Borghi. Mero hopes that somehow this montage will resolve itself into a spirit. It must be a merciful spirit that will return him to his red desert; Arturo. Mero fears death, but only insofar as it represents the deprivation of sense, of memory.

Arturo's strange heat burns suddenly behind him. Hand on his shoulder. Arturo's hand poised: a lovely insect, each digit stained with the colors of a different tattoo, each hand with its own painted eye. They looked at Mero, weighing his mettle. Arturo whispers in his ear, leaden and stifling. "You'll love New York. And before long, I'll join you. No problem. Just stay relaxed. You'll do better if you stay relaxed." Shows him the ticket in its paper folder, tucks it away in Mero's pocket. There was something coronal and sacred in their moment of parting. Mero can barely breathe.

Outside the airplane window now he sees only mountains of clouds jerking by, pillowy towers glistening with stains of bitter sunlight. Mero catches the murmuring of prayers all around him, that soft moving of lips, a warm fluid of plaintive hope rising.

It is all for naught, Mero thinks, asking for forgiveness from such heights. People once gazed upon the fluffy undersides of the clouds and imagined the Kingdom of God lying in store for them atop the swirling wisps. But the aircraft's trajectory has disclosed the nonexistence of a medieval Heaven. Looking over these deserted cloud tops is obscene, he decides. It reveals them somehow naked, bereft of souls. How cruel. But Heaven was always an instrument of cruelty, unconcerned with those marked by tragic fates, a gated community sealed in lofty eternity. Mero wonders: where is Heaven supposed to be, today, if not on the clouds?

His whole body shakes now, his weak grip overcome. Lying stupid and open-palmed next to the glowering cowboy. The cowboy cannot offer protest any more. His face a shriveled gray, he retreats within his own negotiations with an Almighty. It's not just the babies who shriek uncontrollably now. People are losing their shit. The next aisle up from the foreigner, the teeth of a chinless man chatter pitifully. His wife puts her hand over his hairy knuckles and strokes them gently. She has to have enough courage for both of them. Make your peace with this world, and prepare for the next.

Impossibly, the plane's speed seems to be slowing even as the wobbling crescendos. It is coming, ominously, to a stop.

Suddenly, the plane is still. Silent. It is no longer moving. The engines are off. The Boeing is stationary, suspended in mid-air. No one moves a muscle or says a word. People barely breathe. Outside the window is pure white, emptiness. The aircraft is not going down. They seem to somehow be stuck in a cloud bank. The penitents thank their gods in muted whispers. Too soon, in Mero's estimate. There is some ancient power at work here. At this moment, without thinking further about the matter, Mero falls asleep.

Once and never dead, the Two God Ometeotl returns from Omeyocan, Source of All-Life, to the lower heavens, skins of quilted ozone, membranes between skies. The Two God: male and female, the double parent of the great stones' delirium erupts to a sudden vigilance.

Its scarlet masonry glows resplendent against the sky. The bronzed mega-body is taut and muscular, with the arms of an archer, the thighs of a pyramid climber. Ometeotl has hands the size of archipelagos and a grip that can throttle the wind itself. The god peers down through eye-stones one hundred stairflights tall. What is this metal insect suspended amongst the lines of Our ancient palm?

A blood-soaked mist curls around the aircraft's miniscule wings. The god's breath, *spiritus*, a commingling of ten thousand souls, circles the pathetic prayers of the impotent passengers. God of light and dark, Ometeotl's gaze travels on a photon's shadow through the fuselage's dim wiring. These strange mortals with their fruit-fly anxieties, they cannot aspire to the terrible glory of the Eternal! Their miserable cowardice before death mocks the looted treasure houses of Our divine Two Truth. As surely as our *teotl* has given animus, it can hurry the passage of life's shadow across the cloudy reflection of the Mere World.

Mero feels the thump of Arturo's blood, a slumbering heartbeat *veteris vestigia* deep inside, and stupidly believes that he is still dreaming. None of this should be happening. We have no business tracking our filthy exhaust fumes into a god's beloved exile. *Con permiso.* What shabby manners.

Ometeotl finds a snarl of understanding tangled amidst the churning toxins of fear and regret. Who calls out to the Two God Ometeotl? Who disturbs Us in Our Kingdom?

Aha, a Dreamer answers! For an infinite second, the boy beholds the world as the god does: the sky a crystal liquid, still wrinkled with the etchings of Ometeotl's gentle panic, a universe primordially flattened and still trembling with populous life. We wear these sanguine mists as Our glove. We lacquer Earth and Sky onto Our skin as We once painted *teotl* upon the powdered bones of Mictlan. What will become of this wayward insect knocking against the Hibernaculum of our Eternal-All? Little Boeing, do you not understand that you shall return to Us no matter if you live or die today, no matter if you fly or fall?

Seeing the aircraft through the eyes of each zooming photon, Ometeotl tosses Mero through the husk of all Forms; through worlds of burnished turquoise and glittering black stone. The interglossia of unspoken repentance pierces the Mere World with anchor lines, beating hearts imploring a lost Heaven: Return! Each life crying out, too attached to sever the final tether, to turn away forever. They cringe and cling to sentiment, until the moment they beg for Our release: from impoverished mass and matter to enter what lies beyond the planet's ever-vanishing curvature. This is not a plane of Being that answers to pity. And yet . . .

Little Boeing, you are not yet worthy of Our transcendence. You must leave the doorstep of Omeyocan.

A scarlet fingertip awkwardly flicks the miniscule airplane into the cloud swirls. The Boeing catches a stream of warm air and its engines miraculously re-engage. It falls away across the horizon like so many grains of sand.

The soft whir has returned, that soothing noise of lukewarm transience. Am I asleep? thinks Mero. They're moving again. Down the aisle, people whisper to one another, trying to piece together the strange episode. Color has returned to the knuckles of the gray-haired foreigner across from Mero, but he still sits as if petrified, lost in a Black Forest of contemplation. In front of Mero, the two ranchers talk excitedly. They have earnest Midwestern accents and graying pompadour haircuts.

"Did you hear what it was?"

"The stewardess told me how the captains were looking and far-off they see this little speck in the sky. So it's right in the path of the plane, see, just hovering. Radar's going crazy, and boom! That's when the turbulence starts."

"So, like some other aircraft or something? Maybe someone gone off course?"

"Well, that's what they think, right? So they turn the plane to take a different heading, but try as they might, the thing stays right in front, right smack dab in the way of the plane. Like it's moving with us and keeps blocking our way."

"Yeah? Yeah? So then what?"

"So then, we're getting closer, and they start making out what it is—"

"Well, what is it? I mean, what was it?"

"Unbelievable, that's what it was. I mean, I don't believe it, not for one second."

"So what, you gonna tell me or not?"

"Well . . . The stewardess, she overhears the captains saying this big coppery hand just come out of the clouds and scooped us up."

"Shaddup!"

"Her words, not mine. I mean, I didn't see it. Nobody back here did. But she overheard them pilots saying how this hand was huge. Huge and copper-colored."

"Shoot, you stare at the empty sky for long enough you're bound to start seeing things. Mirages and kooky things like that. I bet it happens all the time. Looking at clouds all day's bound to get anyone funny in the head."

"More like all those little bottles what got them funny in the head." Hearty chuckles ensue.

"That stewardess better stop taking them the hard stuff. This whole flying thing ain't no joke, tell you what." Stern agreement between the two ranchers. Throat-chuffing. White noise.

Mero sits back into the thin cushion of his seat, smiling. Next to him the cowboy sleeps, his chin planted squarely on his sternum. The cowboy's presence folds into itself, smelling of aftershave and lanolin and just the faintest stink of pipe tobacco. Mero yawns slightly, and before dozing off again his ears pop. He purrs, and the sleeping cowboy returns a lover's growl, signifying slumbering closeness and nothing more.

He dreams again of Ometeotl, fire engine red against the clouds, outlined with flames of pure glory. Mero wanders among the blood-limned mountain ranges of Omeyocan, exultant and rapturous. He follows blind footsteps across a desert and sees a figure. His wild eyes grip the Heavens, parched lips parting. Mero lucidly touches the marks on his shoulder where Arturo's teeth left a bruise in the shape of a broken circle. It can be hard to fly alone for the first time. But at least the sand has finally gone from his fingers.

MIRROR WRITING

Joanne M. Clarkson

I hold my worries up
against false silver. From
east to west hands
behind glass trace
my glyphs. Into

night windows, I lift
a list of loves
denied, an imprisoned
woman's song. I walk

along a wintered
pond, shedding wants
like stiff gray leaves. Who
swims beneath to
read them? Who
considers spring
real?

And over summer's
mirage, I wave my
failings. Only the
road believes
only the invisible
heals. Oh twin

from my becoming, my left
handed sister who swam
through my moods
from moon to moon, write
back. Ab-
solve me.

MIRROR WRITING: ANTIPHON

I hold your breath my
amniotic sister. It is
never winter here. I
bathe you when wind
steals rain, when
sand exacts
symbols.

Confession is the
purest form of self
seen backwards. I am
your vanity. Come

closest to the glass.
See? There is only
one eye.

WHEN AS CHILDREN WE ACTED MEMORABLY

Zach Powers

The smell of chlorine brings back a memory of the strange cabin on the hill. Each time it is a different memory of a different cabin on a different hill, and once in a valley. It is a memory of brick walls or stacked logs or sheetrock. The windows were high and wide or triple-paned or thick and old and full of distortions. The view was of bald hills or forest or rivers ribboning into the distance. The only constant in the memory is the loose concept of a cabin and the smell of chlorine caught on the air.

The memory comes back, spoken like a song, idealized. My friends, though, were exactly as I recall. I know how they looked, their precise diction, the meaning behind their silences. I remember everything, even as they diminish in the distance.

Ricky's parents installed an above-ground pool the summer after we finished third grade. It never really got warm enough in our town for swimming, so it was the only pool any of us had ever seen, rising conspicuously from the rock-strewn backyard, forming a triangle with the doghouse and the yellow shed. It was made of straight panels, four feet wide, arranged in a jagged oval. I never bothered to count the sides then, to identify the shape more accurately. Dodecagon? Now, years later, it seems like an important piece of information, lost, except maybe in photographs stored in Ricky's parents' closet. If they're still alive. They were Asian, Ricky's family, and the only non-white people in our suburban neighborhood. His father did something for a corporation, earning enough to afford swimming pools and barbecue grills and trips to Caribbean islands in the winter. I remember his father best, again, by a smell. The scent of cigars, over-pungent to the undeveloped sinuses of a child, followed Ricky's father like an olfactory shadow. In the evenings when Ricky's friends came over to swim, he greeted us with a terse hello.

The cigar smell was complemented by that of whiskey on his breath. He was an intangible presence in the room, something I was aware of but couldn't wrap my hands around. A strong desire to hold something paired with the crippling inability to do so.

We settled into a routine, converging on the pool every day for the same set of games, the same races. After swimming, we would dry off with the gauze-like towels provided by Ricky's mother. She would have cookies waiting for us on the porch table, which sat in the one patch of sunlight that reached down between the trees and the roof of the house. The type of cookie changed each day, baked fresh, and the smell of baking is how I best remember Ricky's mother. She was the mother we all flocked to, wishing she was our own. After school we ran to Ricky's house and stayed there until dinnertime, often through it, a half-dozen children huddled around the too-small dining room table. Ricky's mother served us simple food, in nugget or sandwich form, on thin paper plates, and when we were done she whisked away the remnants before we could offer to help clear the table. She taught most of us our fractions. On our birthdays, Ricky's gifts, selected by his mother, were always exactly what we wanted. Later, after our mothers forbade us from going over to Ricky's house, I missed Ricky's mother more than anything. More than the pool, even more than Ricky himself.

That summer we learned to dive—unadvisedly—into the shallow pool. The first awkward bellyflops evolved into graceful needle punctures of the water's surface. We pulled ourselves up just before we reached the bottom, skimming it with our stomachs, bodies held in torpedo shape, letting momentum carry us forward and buoyancy lift us up. Most of us bruised elbows and knees, sometimes a head, but as we got better the injuries became less frequent. Ricky was the proud master of the pool. The undisputed champion of breath-holding competitions, the fastest swimmer, a tenacious Marco and an elusive Polo. He was the first to master diving and the most graceful. It was from him that the rest of us learned the subtleties of the art. With his encouragement we overcame our fear and entered head-first into the water. I remember him by his hair, a black mass, always messy, as if intentionally so. And his stance, proud but relaxed, as he stood, shirtless by the pool, awaiting his turn to dive. Looking back, he was my best friend, though I suspect I am not the only one from our group who would claim the same thing. His absence is a palpable void in the universe. I know that somewhere, in some empty space, he *should* exist. I suppose he does exist, somewhere. What I feel, then, is my own ignorance as to the location of the space he inhabits.

Besides Ricky, the only other childhood friend I remember clearly is Lindsay. She was Ricky's opposite, awkward and flighty. She seemed to stumble with every step, tripping over flat sidewalks and stubbing her toes on anything that poked even an inch out of the ground. Her long blond hair, cobweb thin, was picked up by the lightest breeze and danced around her head like an electric halo. When she got out of the pool, her hair clung so close to her scalp that she looked almost bald. She spoke, when she spoke at all, in a high voice, high even for a young girl. She was the smart one, tasked with looking out for the rest of us. It was her small voice that warned us of oncoming traffic when we were about to dart into the street, or alerted us to the presence of overhead power lines when we swung sticks in mock sword fights. She was like a sister to me and Ricky, a figure of unassailable purity. Given the opportunity, in later years, we would have looked at her differently.

One day in the middle of summer, Lindsay mounted the deck and looked down at the pool. She stood there for a long time. From behind her, those of us waiting our turn to dive urged her to hurry, but she just stood there, gazing into the rippling aquamarine, the lining of the pool lending its hue to the clear, filtered water.

"I see something," said Lindsay.

Before we could ask what she saw, she leapt high off the deck, inverted herself at the apex of her flight, and dove straight down into the water. The angle was too steep. There was no way she could pull up, no way she could avoid smashing her face into the bottom of the pool. She entered with barely a splash. We waited, breath held as if we were underwater. Lindsay did not resurface. Ricky was on the steps. I don't know if it was panic or instinct, or if something called him as it had called Lindsay. He bounded across the platform, and without hesitation, in a near-perfect imitation of Lindsay's dive, followed her into the water. I screamed his name, but he was already submerged. I scrambled up the steps and looked with terror at the bottom of the pool. There was nothing there. No Lindsay. No Ricky. I looked around the yard, trying to discern the nature of the trick, the means by which the two of them had perpetrated this magnificent illusion. But they were nowhere. The others, standing on the porch, mouths agape, looked at me. I shook my head.

"They are not there," I said. "There is no one in the pool as if there never had been. The water is perfectly clear and empty like the sky on a cloudless afternoon."

My friends nodded their heads sagely, as if they had understood something beyond the words I had spoken.

I looked back down into the water. Something seemed to move at the bottom of the pool, like seaweed waving in ocean currents, directly below where my two friends had disappeared. Before I could think anything, unable to think at all, I found myself making the same vertical dive into the water, aimed directly at the kelp-like something below. I opened my eyes wide and tried to scream but produced only bubbles. The floor of the pool rushed up. I swallowed a gulp of the medicinal water. I hit the bottom. But it wasn't hard. I passed into it as through a thick gel and floated there. The substance was warm and comforting, like the embrace of Ricky's mother, like the smell of fresh baked cookies. The longer I was inside it the more I relaxed, until, at the last moment, I felt like my mind left my body, and with it went all stresses and agitations. And, as a blank slate, I entered the cabin.

I dropped onto a mattress covered with a down comforter. When I tried to wipe the water out of my eyes, I realized that I was completely dry, dressed in comfortable clothes not quite like the current fashions but not completely different either, a sweater and pants I could imagine Ricky's father wearing when he was a child. I propped myself up on the bed. The room around me was the size of an average living room, and besides the bed, I saw a kitchen table, a sink, and a sofa. Ricky and Lindsay stood looking out a yellow-curtained window.

"Where are we?" I asked.

"In a cabin," said Ricky, "with snow outside, white and glistening in the sun like a distant field of diamonds."

I half-hopped, half-stumbled off the bed and joined them at the window. The hill was bare of trees, and as far as could be seen undisturbed snow covered an undulating landscape, more hills like the one on which we found ourselves, but the others just a bit lower. I touched the window and felt the cold move from the glass to my fingertips. A circle of condensation formed where Ricky's mouth pressed near the pane. I looked at my clothes more closely. They were tailored for the environment, the sweater heavy and the pants thickly padded. The pattern on the middle of the sweater was of interlocking triangles, white on teal, the colors like the surface of the pool. Ricky and Lindsay were similarly dressed.

Ricky went to the door. He jiggled the knob back and forth, but it would not turn. He returned to the window and tried to push it open, but it was frozen shut. I joined him in attempting to raise it, but still it would not move. My hands felt numb where they had pushed against the glass, and I rubbed them together. Lindsay stood beside the bed, looking up at a point on the ceiling directly above it. A wisp of white energy hung there, like a tiny version of the Northern Lights. After watching it for many minutes, I realized it was the same as the kelp-like thing I had seen at the bottom of the pool. I had fallen into the room from that point. It was the portal.

That first cabin is the one I remember best. We spent much time there, inspecting each corner, the sparse furnishings, the grain of the wood-paneled wall. We tried to force open the door, each of the windows. None of them would budge, so we returned our attention to the interior. The circular rug in the center of the room, made from a coarse brown material, sprouting fuzz all over, was woven with a design of random green triangles. Leaning close, I first noticed, from the fabric, the smell of chlorine that would later define the whole experience. Once I had smelled it, I couldn't ignore it. It became overpowering, forcing itself up my nostrils, pounding inside my head. I grew dizzy. I saw that my friends were experiencing something similar, staggering under the attack of an unseen assailant.

"I think we should leave," said Ricky. "My head is spinning around inside itself and I feel the walls reaching toward me with invisible hands."

"But how do we leave?" I asked.

"I am not exactly sure how we got here," said Lindsay. "It was as if we were pulled in, beckoned by an unspeaking voice."

Ricky nodded. "We will return as we came, through the spot of light on the ceiling, which was, before, on the bottom of the pool."

He climbed onto the bed, bounced slowly at first, then faster and higher, extending his arms straight out, spinning in tight circles as if dancing a dervish. Light descended like a liquid and surrounded him, suspending him in the air halfway between the bed and the ceiling. He spun there for a moment, wrapped in light, floating. Once per revolution he faced me, his expression slack, eyes closed, the countenance of sleep. His turning slowed, stopped. He opened his eyes and they were nothing but whites. Tilting back his head, he rose toward the ceiling. The light grew too bright to look at, filled the whole of the cabin with whiteness, washing out even the outlines of our bodies. I groped in blindness for Lindsay, to stabilize myself against the dizziness, to assuage my fear, but I found nothing. The floor beneath me lost substance. My body dissolved, turned to mist. I screamed with the mouth, throat, lungs I no longer had. All that came was silence, then gurgling. My head broke the surface of the pool. I gasped for air, though my chest was free from the burning sensation of held breath. The familiar sights of Ricky's back yard surrounded me—trees and slatted fence and the rough red-brown brick of the house. I was back in my swimsuit. Ricky and Lindsay stood with me in the water. Like any three points, we formed a triangle, but this one was special, the distance between us and the subtleties of the angles. I can't explain how, but I knew its specialness in the same way I knew to dive into the water and Ricky knew the way to return us home.

In the world outside the cabin, I had expected time to stand still. I had expected our friends to be waiting for us, waiting to hear the story of where we had been and what we had seen. I imagined them sitting on the deck, feet dangling in the water, faces to the sun. But the shadows had shifted to cover the yard and our friends were gone. There was no sign that they had ever been there. Usually we left a trail of towels and toys in our wake. But the surface of the back porch was empty, even swept free of fallen leaves.

"You're back," Ricky's mother spoke to us from the porch. "I was worried you would not return, as you spent much time in the cabin, long enough, surely, to feel its effects, the vertigo that overtakes you, that sends you spinning, spinning, spinning."

"Why could we not stay longer?" asked Ricky.

"It will get easier each time. It is a dangerous place, the cabin, but I know better than to forbid you to visit. You three form an interesting triangle. Maybe you can conquer that place. Maybe you can open the door."

She held out three towels toward us.

"Come," she said, "have some cookies. I have just finished baking them."

Inside, fresh cigar smoke filled the house. I heard the sounds of a baseball game coming from the television in the living room. We passed Ricky's father and he looked at us, would not look away from us. I'm sure kept staring in our direction even after we were out of sight, but he did not speak a word. In the kitchen, wrapped in the thin white towels, we ate cookies. My thoughts left the strange place we had visited and turned to the activities of the evening, the cartoons to be watched and video games to be played. I tried to speak of such things to Ricky and Lindsay but they remained silent, in their eyes the vacant look I had seen on Ricky's face as he hung above the bed in the cabin.

Our other friends, those who had watched us dive and disappear into the water, didn't come to Ricky's house again. When we saw them in the neighborhood, they would greet us like usual, sometimes join us in games, but something was strange. They never referred to the event, even when prompted, to the point that I am unsure if they remembered it at all. But they knew something. There was a reason why they wouldn't return to the pool, why their mothers shied away from us or took their children's hands if we approached. Sometimes when they talked I could hardly understand them. Ricky knew it, too. He distanced himself from everyone but me and Lindsay. I didn't mind, because I could lay more exclusive claim to the boy I considered my best friend. I could finally feel like the title went both ways, at least for a while. The power of our secret brought us together. I loved being in possession of the secret more than I cared for the secret itself. I loved our triangle more than the cabin.

On the day after our first visit to the cabin, we had returned to Ricky's back yard. We crept to the edge of the pool and looked down for the glowing spot on the bottom. It was there, in the same place, distorted by the rippling water, which was agitated by a gentle but ceaseless wind. This time I did not feel the compulsion to dive. That first time, I had felt beckoned, like I was being asked an important question that could only be answered through action, and so I had entered the pool not out of decision but out of instinct. Now I felt, at most, curious, though in the posture of my friends, the way they leaned just a little bit forward, I saw that they were drawn to the bottom as strongly as before, and I knew that I would follow them. Eventually it became habitual—the more we visited the cabin the more we felt we had to visit, until it came to seem essential, at least for the other two.

Ricky dove into the water first, as he would each time we returned. As he neared the bottom, white light, flowing like milk in the water, surrounded him, faded, and he was no longer there. I let Lindsay go next. I watched as she, too, disappeared, and I stood there for a while in the steady breeze over the empty pool. My body trembled. It was not that I felt afraid, exactly. But I was already beginning to feel out of place, my point of the triangle obtuse to the acuteness of my friends. I felt necessary for the shape, as Ricky's mother had described it, but standing there alone, a point, without length or width, I doubted the necessity of the shape. They were already there, Ricky and Lindsay, and I was not, and sadly, it seemed not to matter. But my doubt was overpowered by the pending adventure and the desire to be with my friends, so I dove to the bottom of the pool, into the light, through the gelatinous something between the pool and the cabin, and I fell softly onto the bed in the corner.

The dimensions were roughly the same, but this cabin was constructed and furnished differently from the first. The walls were papered in a tacky flower pattern, the pinks too bright and the green of the leaves flat, lifeless. Against the far wall was a kitchenette with a small stove and refrigerator, microwave and toaster, a row of cabinets a few feet above the counter. A sofa, upholstered in fabric that looked to be selected specifically to clash with the wallpaper, occupied the center of the room, and it faced toward an old television set like the one on which Ricky's father watched sports, where the roar of the crowd came out robotically from built-in speakers. A rabbit-eared antenna sat on the TV, prongs angled in such a way that if they were connected across the top they would form a familiar triangle. Ricky and Lindsay were sitting on the couch watching a black and white movie. The actress on screen spoke with over-careful diction.

I went to the front door, thick and old and wooden, and tried to turn the knob, but it didn't even wiggle. Through the windows I saw tree trunks, almost atop the cabin, and looking up I could just catch a glimpse of the green forest canopy as it faded to shadow very nearby, the thick woods blocking the sun and making the afternoon feel like dusk. I went through the cabinets and found all sorts of food, some canned, some fresh. All of it looked newly bought. The same was true of the refrigerator. I took with me three apples and joined my friends on the couch and watched the incomprehensible middle of the movie with the strange-talking starlet. We finished our apples. Ricky stood.

"We should probably leave," he said, "before the vertiginous effects of this place again take hold."

Lindsay nodded. "I agree. Already I feel my balance altered, as if I were on the corner of myself, just before the tipping point."

As before, Ricky climbed onto the bed. He bounced, then floated, then disappeared in light. The light spread through the whole room. I watched the ugly walls as they were bleached into nonexistence, and I was warmed inside by the thought of homecoming. We were again in the pool, again formed our triangle. I tried to note the specific angles, to be able later to sketch the triangle on paper, but the exact shape eluded me.

On the deck, Ricky and Lindsay were overtaken by shivering as the wind, stronger now than before we left, licked across the wetness of their skin and carried away warmth with the evaporating water. I did not feel cold, however. I was aware of the wind, but to me it delivered fresh, familiar air. The whole time I had been in the cabin I had felt short of breath. Now, back home, I could again breathe normally. So the cold did not bother me and the faint prickling on my skin was like waking up.

Ricky's mother gazed out at us from the kitchen window. I thought she looked sad, but I couldn't tell because her face was dark behind the glass, which reflected back, over her, a faint image of the slatted fence. She saw me looking and moved away from the window. Moments later she came onto the porch with cookies that steamed in the cold air. I bit into a cookie as Ricky and Lindsay toweled off. The taste was of warmth more than flavor. As I chewed my first mouthful, Ricky's mother hugged me, quickly, as if she didn't want the action to be seen, and then went back inside. It was the last batch of cookies she baked for us. Ricky and Lindsay never seemed to notice their absence. But the cookies were all I could think of. How I hungered for them, more and more, each time they didn't appear.

We developed a routine for the rest of that summer. The three of us would gather at Ricky's house after lunch, already in our swimsuits. I didn't see Ricky's mother anymore as we passed through the house and out the back door to the pool. Sometimes I saw her in the kitchen window. Each time her figure looked darker, until it was nothing but a silhouette, and toward the end she disappeared completely.

Ricky would lead us into the water. Then Lindsay. By the time I arrived, the two of them were already engaged in whatever activity that particular version of the cabin had to offer. Sometimes we just stared out the window, amazed by the many landscapes the world had to offer. Sometimes we watched TV. The programs were different each time, always old, films and sitcoms representing, in black and white, a reality I could not recognize. I wonder now what my childhood reality would have looked like to a viewer in the distant future. Once we found the cabin furnished only with a ping pong table. We spent the whole day there, returning to the pool long after evening had set in. Once, on a round table in the middle of the room, we found three pairs of binoculars, placed carefully as the corners of a triangle, and out the windows, alighting in a sparse forest, flocks of birds of every imaginable species. Once we found the floor covered with the scattered pieces of a massive jigsaw puzzle. We spent the afternoon assembling the edges, but when we returned the next day, both the puzzle and our progress were gone.

It was the last week of summer vacation. My afternoon visits to the pool were replaced by shopping trips with my mother to buy school supplies. She walked far ahead of me through the store, slinging items into her basket without asking me if I needed them. Pulling a staple remover from the shelf, she pressed it shut several times, the device like a biting mouth, before she placed it atop the pile in her basket. I followed her into another aisle, this one completely filled with pens, hung tightly-spaced on the pegboard, endless variations on color and ink and tip. I didn't see my mother stop in front of me and bumped into her. She was smiling at Ricky's father, Ricky beside him. Ricky hunched his shoulders and shifted his eyes away, and looked, just this once, small and meek. I tried to smile at him, but I couldn't. I didn't recognize in the boy before me the elements that made up my friend. I might not have recognized him at all if not for the scent of his father's cigars filling up the aisle.

My mother greeted Ricky's father warmly. She seemed not to notice Ricky. I realized for the first time that she didn't know Ricky as well as Ricky's mother knew me. Maybe all my mother knew of him was this timid boy before her now, eyes downcast, hair unusually neat and parted. She asked Ricky's father how his wife was doing.

"She is as expected. I can feel her diminishing, falling away to a distant source of gravity that stretches her thinner and thinner."

"I understand," said my mother. "I know she did not volunteer for such a thing, but it is admirable the way she bears it. I wish her well, and if I do not see her again, please let her know that I will think of her, for instance, when I look in a mirror or lift a somewhat heavy object."

Ricky's father shook his head in an exaggerated motion. "It is not you who needs to express gratitude. Goodbye."

He moved out of the aisle. Ricky lingered for a moment, but he would not raise his eyes to mine. Eventually, he too walked away, and I caught my mother scowling after him with a look of disgust on her face, like a slap, that in later years would be directed at me. I followed her through the rest of the store as she bought school supplies as if for herself.

On the last Friday of summer vacation I found myself free. I met Ricky in his backyard. We dangled our feet in the pool, and I recalled for a moment the simple pleasure of swimming, which we had forgotten, distracted by our trips to the cabin, so I slid into the water and swam laps until Lindsay arrived. She stood by the edge of the pool and looked around, slowly, pausing sometimes on the landmarks of the backyard—the large stone by the fence, the yellow tool shed, the doghouse that had housed no dogs of which I knew. I swam to the platform and splashed her with water. She laughed, and kicked a retaliatory splash at my face. I shielded my eyes, so I did not see Ricky cannonball into the pool, soaking Lindsay completely and sending a wave over the top of my head.

I was the last, as usual, to the cabin. In the room, other than the bed, there were three chairs, and nothing else, arranged in the shape of a familiar triangle. The walls were bare sheetrock, painted white. No curtains hung over the windows, only cheap Venetian blinds, retracted all the way to the top. The floor was tiled in one-foot-wide black squares with no gaps between, like in the halls of our school. I slid off the bed and looked out the window. Grassy hills spread away from the cabin, their edges clear against the clear sky. Ricky and Lindsay already occupied two of the chairs. I took the third.

We talked. For many hours, we talked of everything we knew. We expelled the whole limited knowledge of our young existences. A story from one of us led seamlessly into a story from another. I felt a pleasant tightness in my chest, a euphoric relaxation of my limbs, warmth all over, blanketed in the company of these, my friends. Toward the end of our conversation, we recounted the discovery of the light in the pool, and we took turns recalling our many visits to the cabin. It was Ricky's turn.

"We arrived," he said, "and found three chairs in the center of a white room with a black floor. The arrangement of the chairs was familiar, in a triangle that was not quite equilateral, but not so different that I could name the angles. We sat and talked for many hours, then we opened the door and left."

The door, set in a white frame, was a featureless black rectangle with a brass doorknob glinting suspiciously halfway up its surface. We rose from the chairs as one and moved to the door, maintaining the shape of our triangle as we went. Ricky gripped the knob, turned. The smell of grass rushed through the open door, chasing away that of chlorine. I blinked in the sudden sunlight. Ricky stepped outside as if into his own backyard, then Lindsay, but I remained motionless, unable to will my feet to follow. Reaching across the threshold, I grabbed Ricky by the shoulder, but he pulled away from me. My hand slid down his arm to his hand, which I gripped as if to shake. He looked back, not at me, but at our joined hands, and I could not recognize in the boy before me the one I called my friend. I released him. As Ricky walked from the cabin, the space between us, ever growing, felt more real, more solid, than the air it was made from, the distance farther than the paces counted from there to here. The room flashed white behind me. When I looked, only one of the chairs remained.

I slid the chair over and sat in the open doorway and watched Ricky and Lindsay run off over the smooth green hills. They ran with limitless energy, surging up each slope, disappearing over each crest, only to emerge again on the face of a hill even more distant. Toward the horizon the hills grew gray, the farthest completely desaturated and indistinguishable from the sky. I thought to follow, to sprint after, calling out for my friends to wait, but instead I sat, silent. I don't know why I didn't follow. I missed them immediately, felt deflated, empty, but I missed them like they had died, a hopeless sort of emptiness that no action could relieve. The people they had been, the children who were my friends, were gone, irrevocably, and those two I watched running away from me were other people altogether, strangers. They crested the farthest hill, stick figures against a backdrop of clouds, and I heard, even from this distance, their laughing, joyous, primal, as they slid, finally, from view.

I closed the door and twisted the lock. They would not be back, I was sure of that. I sealed the cabin, pulled the blinds, feeling the whole time very much like I was burying myself. In the dark, the glowing spot on the ceiling looked more solid, less wisplike, and it called to me, stronger than it ever had. I realized my trips to the cabin weren't for the cabin itself, or for the sense of adventure, but for the solidity of friendship, and now that my friends were gone I was called to a home where I might, eventually, make new friends to replace those I had lost.

I jumped on the bed, mimicking Ricky's movements as best I could, bouncing, higher and higher, impossibly high, lifted by an unknown force. As I spun it felt like the cabin revolved around me, like I was suddenly the center of the universe. The spot on the ceiling spread, light descended and enveloped me, a warm feeling like a towel that has been resting in sunlight. Whiteness filled the room, and as it faded I felt the water of the pool wash around me, the scent of chlorine overpowering. I climbed out of the water, but found no towel waiting for me. I stood there for a long time, letting the sun dry me, in a wind that carried unfamiliar smells from distant places.

It was quiet in Ricky's house, absent the familiar sound of the television. I called out to Ricky's mother. I needed to tell her Ricky was gone. I needed to tell her everything. I smelled cigars and turned to find, looming over me, the whole mass of Ricky's father. He looked at me like he didn't know me, like he had never before seen a child. He knelt so that his eyes were at the level of mine, but I cannot recall his face, and remember instead darkness, a black cloud of cigar smoke in the shape of a man. He gripped me, painfully, by the shoulders, as if to affirm the solidity of his form.

"You're back," said Ricky's father. "You had the infinite world awaiting you outside the unlocked door, and yet you return."

I saw Ricky's mother behind him. She was in a wheelchair, withered, skinny to the bone, gray-haired where once it had been black. Her hands, nimble in the preparation of meals and the baking of cookies, were now gnarled, fingers hooked toward palms, knuckles swollen. The skin of her face sagged, and the only recognizable thing about her, amidst the loose flesh, was her eyes, which looked at me, I now realized, with gratitude. I broke myself free from the grasp of Ricky's father and embraced her. She hugged me back, but weakly—so weakly I started to cry for everything that had ever been lost.

I said to Ricky's mother, "They ran from the door, across hills like a green rolling sea, until in the distance they disappeared. They did not wave goodbye, and I do not think they will think of this place again."

"Nor should you," said Ricky's father. "You are not welcome here, and I know not what awaits you in your own home. It was not supposed to happen this way. Look at her." He thrust a finger toward Ricky's mother. "She is frail as an autumn leaf. You came back, and so this little bit remains. Now she will stay withered and the rest of us will age and the promise of eternity grows more distant with each step you take in this world. What have you done?"

I was too young to understand it, and even now it is unclear what was at stake. Ricky's mother knew she had to let us go but loved us too much to do so. By coming back, I let her have both: the holding on and the release. I worry sometimes, though, that maybe it was neither.

Ricky's mother reached after me as I opened the front door and stepped outside. Before I ran from the door, down the street, parallel to the line of similar houses, I spoke to her for the last time.

"I bounced on the bed and spun in the air and vanished in the light."

THE COCA-COLA LADY

Wendy Patrice Williams

This time Dad came home with the Coca-Cola Lady. Not the usual old fans, lamps, and radios that he picks up in order to fix but a life-sized, stand-up woman like a giant paper doll. He carried her into the house under his left arm and disappeared down the basement where he puts all his junk.

I came upon her later that afternoon when I ran downstairs for the pretzel tin during a TV commercial. I got scared at first. Who was standing in the doorway at the bottom of the steps? But halfway down, as I turned on the light, I could see it was her—eyes twinkling, arms offering a tray on which two words were painted in red with a wavy dash in-between: COCA-COLA.

As I came back holding the pretzel tin against my stomach, I measured us. She was a head taller than me, closer to my mom's height, and her lips were red-red like Cousin Judy's. A one-piece yellow bathing suit covered her boobs and crotch and her legs were tan the way my legs got tan—with gold in them: not the usual skinny sticks you see on models but fleshy like mine—the kind Dad liked. She was friendly-looking, regular, not like the photos on Dad's workshop walls. I liked her but for some reason felt embarrassed that she was there. Mounting the stairs two by two, I felt her watching the backs of my thighs.

Later that evening I heard Dad calling me. I was in the middle of watching *Gunsmoke* and didn't want to miss it. I ran to the top of the stairs and yelled, "What?" An Irish tenor was holding a high note on his radio, and I wondered if he could hear me.

"Come on down a minute, I've got something to show you."

"OK," I said, descending the stairs, gritting my teeth because I was missing my show. The Coca-Cola Lady was not there in the doorway, and I wondered where she'd gone.

Dad leaned over the lathe at the far end of the workshop, orange sparks flying out to either side as he sharpened the blades of my skates. Above him, pinned onto the cabinet door, was Brunette Lady. I felt her peering down at me. She was completely naked, kneeling on a fluffy, black rug, with her boobs hanging way down because she was leaning over. Her eyes knew some weird secret—as if she could get you in a lot of trouble if she told—and she smiled as if she had just played a trick on somebody.

As I came up alongside him, he turned to me, one of my blue ice skates in his hands.

"Pretty good, huh?"

He handed it to me, and I ran my finger over the edge of the blade. "Yeah," I said, even though ragged jags of metal grabbed my flesh. He handed me the other skate and turned off the whirling metal wheel.

"Take these upstairs and show your mother."

A metallic smell stung my nostrils as I stared down at my skate blades. They were bright silver now, transformed from the dull gray they'd turned after last winter's use.

"Thanks Dad," I said. As I turned to go up the stairs, I spotted the yellow bathing suit of Coca-Cola Lady at the back of the recreation room.

Hi, Coca-Cola Lady, I silently greeted her.

The next night when I came into the kitchen for supper, there was Coca-Cola Lady. She was propped in the corner between the places where my brother, Will, and I sat. Mom stood at the sink, pouring the steaming spaghetti into a strainer. Dad sat at the table, his shoulders large beneath the dark-blue work shirt. Will slid in past Coca-Cola Lady, and I sat down next to her. No one mentioned her. She was the kind of thing one just didn't talk about.

When I saw the cardboard tube next to Dad's plate at the table, I knew it was going to be one of *those* dinners. At the end of each month, Dad got a new calendar from his boss. My stomach squeezed tight like a wooden block clamped by the jaws of a vise. I held my breath as he slid another one of his pin-up queens out of her cylinder.

"Introducing Mrs. Claus," Dad said as he unrolled his latest scroll.

He smiled his bad boy smile at me. Now someone was wringing my stomach like a washcloth.

"It's for December," he said, "Christmas, get it?"

"Yeah, Dad," Will blurted, so he'd shut up. She was blonde, wore a red Santa hat with a white pom-pom on top—that was all—and kneeled on a white polar bear skin. Her boobs were huge like Aunt Fay's. The bear's head lay beside her, its teeth growling.

"I sure wouldn't mind finding her in my stocking Christmas Day," Dad said. "Some boobs, heh Mom?" I kept my head down, shoveling in forkfuls of noodles, jamming in huge wads of buttered Italian bread. Mom and Will stuffed themselves, too.

Coca-Cola Lady did not approve of Mrs. Claus. She thought she should at least be wearing a bathing suit.

Really, I agreed.

And, Coca-Cola Lady said, *she shouldn't be at the supper table.*

Neither should you, I said.

"So Mom, what d'ya think?" Dad asked. "She's a beauty, eh?"

"Anybody want any more sauce?" Mom said, getting up from the table.

Dad rolled up the scroll and slid it back into its container as she ladled more steaming tomato sauce on his meatballs.

It's over, I said to the Coca-Cola Lady. Will and I kicked each other under the table between sips of iced tea from huge tinted glasses.

When Dad pulled out the old stogie from his chest pocket, my stomach relaxed. Mom didn't let him smoke at the table. "Gonna go watch the news," he announced, rising from his chair. Will asked to be excused and jumped up, squeezing past the Coca-Cola Lady, then me.

I felt frozen to my seat. For some reason, I couldn't leave Mom alone with the Coca-Cola Lady while she cleaned up. I offered to dry the dishes. As usual, Mom said, no, that I'd have my own dishes soon enough, so instead, I sponged off the table.

You think he likes me better than her, don't you? Coca-Cola Lady asked.

No way, I tell her.

Dad clomped back.

"Nothing much on. Call me for the *Untouchables* at eight, will ya, Mom?" he said. Then he grabbed Coca-Cola Lady around the waist and carried her down the cellar steps. I thought of that blonde lady kicking her legs and struggling to get out of King Kong's grip as he hung off the Empire State Building.

I never knew where Coca-Cola Lady would pop up next. She might be near Dad's engraving machine or next to the furnace or tucked into the corner with all the fishing poles. Dad moved her around. She usually hung out in the cellar though. Sometimes, when I made sawdust pies in my play kitchen, I planted her nearby for company, but whenever friends came over I made sure she was out of sight. I couldn't bear them making fun of her.

One night there was nothing to do, so I figured I'd shoot some BBs. I turned a cardboard box onto its side, set it on the table saw, and leaned the bottom up against the wall. Then I lined up nails just so on the inside of the box, balancing the gray-blue shafts on their flat, wobbly heads. I called it my Sharp Shootin' Gallery and wished there were moving plastic chicks or ducks to shoot at. Nearby stood Coca-Cola Lady. I moved her so I wouldn't pock her up with ricochets. Dad might be mad about that.

Standing away from the target at the foot of the stairs, I broke the gun in half over my knee to load it. As I poured the BBs into the hole, the copper-colored balls disappeared one by one into the gun barrel. I loved the click-click sound they made as they bumped against each other. Then I closed the gun and rested the handle against my shoulder. I squinted my left eye, sighting the target. Hold it steady, I told myself. Then, I let the nail drift slightly out of the sight. When it drifted back in, POW, I blew it off the map.

What do you think of that, Coca-Cola Lady? I thought, looking over at her. She was smiling.

I rarely missed. Sometimes the BB ricocheted off the nail, and I heard it go clink-clink-clink as it bounced off Dad's machinery. I knocked off the last nail and walked up to my Sharp Shootin' Gallery. The BBs looked pretty, shining in their cardboard craters.

I don't remember how we got started firing at the Brunette Lady. I guess we shot at her because she was at the end of a long aisle—perfect firing range. And because there were already some BB holes in her head.

The Coca-Cola Lady watched Will and me from behind.

"I'm aiming for the left eye, Mand," he said, "See if I don't nail it."

Whack, the BB hit a nearby cabinet and ricocheted, clink, into the jigsaw. A tiny tear appeared in her eyelid.

"A hundred points!" he said.

"I'll go for the other," I said. Maybe I could hit it dead center. Lining it up in the sight, I let 'er drift and fired. Whack, straight into the eyeball.

"Bull's eye!" I shouted, "two hundred points!"

We shot her nose up, then her mouth and her chin. After we nailed her earrings, there was nothing else to do but go for the boobs. They were practically calling out to be shot.

"A thousand points for this one," I called, aiming at one of her nipples. They didn't look anything like Mom's, which were small with hard tips that stuck out. They were that way, she said, because Will and I bit on them so much when we were babies. Brunette Lady's nipples were large, flat and soft looking. Easy targets. Whack, the BB tore a hole into one so you could see the gold wood behind it peeking through. How weird, I thought, that she was all shot up and smiling at the same time.

Will nailed the other nipple and after shooting them up some more, Mom called us for lunch. As I passed Coca-Cola Lady on the way to the stairs, I noticed something had changed. She smiled as though she had a secret that she'd tell on me if I didn't watch out. My stomach turned; I ran away from her up the stairs. When I came down the cellar again after lunch to do some more shooting, I turned Coca-Cola Lady to the wall.

When my best friend Bonnie was over, we often played downstairs in my playhouse. It was really my mother's side of the cellar, but Dad made part of it into a play-kitchen with a table, a sideboard, some shelves and a toy refrigerator and stove. He had built the furniture himself. Bonnie and I pretended to use Mom's washing machine.

One day I led Bonnie past Mom's side into the big cellar room and flicked on the fluorescent light. Coca-Cola Lady stared out from the edge of the darkness. Her face seemed like a mask that didn't belong to her. I motioned to the wall of photos, wondering what Bonnie would think. On the cream-colored plasterboard hung Christmas cards Mom collected over the years along with photos Dad pinned up of lots of Dirty Girls. Photos of women naked and smiling. It was odd to see them alongside the sparkling glitter of the cards.

Bonnie pointed her long, skinny arm at a photo. "Wow," she said, "look at those boobs!" I felt ashamed. She sounded just like my father.

"And look at this one with the fur around her wrists and ankles."

They're just pictures, I snapped at Bonnie in my mind, wanting her to shut up. She wasn't acting at all the way I expected her to. Why didn't she think they were bad?

She stood right next to the wall now, staring hard at one of the photos. "Look, Mand," Bonnie said, pointing to the one I called Red Girl. "She's got your color hair."

"Her hair is red like carrots," I told her, wanting to call her stupid. "Mine is like copper pennies. C'mon." I marched her out of there and flicked off the light.

Later, after Bonnie went home, I went back downstairs to see Red Girl. Behind her, a sky-blue, satiny curtain shimmered. She looked like she was holding her breath. Her lips were all bunched up to give a kiss the way Aunt Bev did. I scrunched my nose remembering her stiff, dry peck. Red Girl was shoving her boobs up and out. It made me think of a drawer pulled all the way out so you could look more easily for whatever you wanted. I wanted to cover her with that blue satin curtain. The words underneath the photo read, "WHATEVER YOU WANT." I turned away, feeling Coca-Cola Lady's eyes on my back as I left.

I see you, Mandy, I heard her say.

One evening walking home from ice skating on the frozen river, my blue skates hanging over my shoulder, I saw Coca-Cola Lady in front of our house. I couldn't believe she was out there for everyone to see. Her face stared out at me from over the rim of one of those industrial-sized garbage cans. How could Dad throw her out? Her head leaned slightly back and a thick crease ran across her neck as if someone had punched her hard with a boxing glove. She's dead, I thought. How did it happen? I wanted to find out, but I couldn't ask my parents about her. Coca-Cola Lady was just something you didn't talk about.

We can fix her, I thought excitedly. But I knew that I couldn't really bring her back into the house. It wasn't like when I found my stuffed animals in the garbage and rescued them. I imagined jumping into the garbage can and pulling a lid over both our heads.

"Bye, Coca-Cola Lady," I said, looking into her soft brown eyes. It was suppertime, and I had to get in. I headed up the driveway, skate blade banging into my chest.

You'll be alone down there now, I heard her say, *all alone with the Dirty Girls.*

My chest burned hearing her words. I rushed back and faced her, hands balled into fists.

Fix me, she begged.

How? I pleaded. *I can't make that crease go away.*

Try.

It's too late, I told her, my head bowed.

I don't see you, Mandy, Coca-Lady said. *I don't see you anymore.*

I shoved her head down into the can and ran up the driveway. As I opened the back door, tears in my eyes, I imagined the garbage men finding her in the morning. They snickered, jabbing each other with their elbows.

Don't laugh at her, I said to them as I slammed the porch door. *She's not a Dirty Girl.* But all they heard was the deafening grind of the garbage truck's machinery.

ONE FLESH IN FLORUIT

Molly English

In October she will feel for the first time through someone else's fingers.

But before that, she will be married under gold leaves, very early in the morning, to a man named Judah whom she loves. She won't wear shoes and neither will he. When the time comes, their breath will be sea fog and their lips the ships that navigate through it.

All of the formalities in magic or science occur after she says, "I do."

I'm told the surgery is simple. The doctors sit on the porch and smoke cigarettes while the spiders do most of the work.

The spiders themselves are too small to see, and they don't itch because of the drugs. So, instead of scratching, Honeymooners lie in the grass tying rubber bands around their fingers. Honeymooners watch skin go from red to blue while the spiders rework the wires in their brains. Once they've built nests inside, the spiders send mail across bodies, back and forth, forever.

I once asked a doctor how this works: spiders in a dead brain, when souls go to heaven.

"Well, they keep doing their job," the doctor told me. He took a drag of his cigarette and kicked the dirt. "They're machines, you know, not like us. They're happy doing the same thing forever, even if it's sending blank signals."

"They're happy?"

"No. You know what I mean: they stay in there forever."

Doctors don't like me because I worry too much about that girl who will be married in October.

I asked, "Forever? Don't they break down?"

"Never."

During the surgery, up on the porch and through cigarette smoke, I'm told. The doctors look like fathers and mothers. The men wear jeans and scowls, and the women wear old hats. They cry sometimes out of love.

In reality, the spiders are more their children than the Honeymooners are. But the doctors look like parents anyway.

When, after their surgery, the girl and Judah hold hands, it will feel backwards. There will be a few seconds of fumbling.

Whosethumbiswhose?

This is a problem of proprioception.

They will slow down and work together, interrogating proper places in form and in space for appendages with unclear loyalties. Fingers under his control that are hers, and hers that are his under her control, and each one a valid excuse to forget: this is easy.

The final product is origami with too many incorrect folds.

Theywillholdhandsdownthepath,feelingbackwards.

The doctors see too much of me. After school, I walk through the woods along the river and meet them in their spots on the porch. By the time I'm there, I have mud on my shoes and they won't let me in. Sometimes we speak on the porch. Sometimes in the ferns where I sit cross-legged and he or she stands.

Once, I asked a doctor, "What about asthma?"

He said, "What *about* asthma?"

I said, "Judah has asthma."

He picked up a feather fallen from an owl's nest and for a moment, his cigarette hand was a carrier of two things. Then, he put one in his pocket, and the other on the ground, rubbing it in the dirt with his sandals.

"You'll have to warn him when he's having an attack." The doctor was serious about this. I think he might have looked worried.

"How will I know?"

"You will. Just remember to warn him. Or he'll die."

"So I'll feel the attack?"

"You'll feel everything he feels. And he'll feel everything you feel. You know how this works." The Doctors see too much of me, so after this they usually say things like: "These are questions for your mother."

So, to them, I say things like: "My mother doesn't know. She's not fixed with my dad."

And to me, they say, "That's a shame. Your poor family."

And I think but don't say,

I think we're okay.

Intime,lovemakingwillbecomeselfish.

The two will walk together to the pond that, like glass, sings call-and-response with the sky.

Shewillexperiencethewaterfirst,becausehejumpsin.

Butsubmerged,Judahonlyfeelsthegoldleavesturningbrownunderher feetandthe wayherlonghairtickleshernakedshoulders. There's a breeze.

He'll motion with his hand for her to join him, and she will feel his muscles tense to make the movement. Likewise, he feels her throat make the words "I'm coming."

They will wrap their fists up in knots of willow tree hairs and their bodies will change the temperature of the water, ifonlyveryslightly. They will touch each other, but in reality, onlytouchthemselves.

They'llthinkit'sallsoromanticandpassionate. And it's true.

I've always wanted to feel what it's like to feel like you.

Eventuallyshe'lllearn.

She'llmisshistouch.

Thenforgethistouch.

And it'll all become so selfish.

When the water finally settles, and they float side by side. The only ripples will be from two heartbeats. A shape like infinity will spread to the bank and make the littleflowersshudder.

Once or twice I asked, "Can I watch you do it?"

The doctors didn't like that. For the longest time they told me, "No."

No, because it's really personal to get fixed.

But on a day when I came in the rain, one of the woman doctors took pity on me. She saw the beads of water and sweat so close to falling from the ends of my hair and said, "Yes."

Yes, but be quiet.

It was late September and the leaves were already greenish gold. So, that too.

At the birth of their first child, she will stain the grass red and drink water through a string in her arm. The doctors in their jeans and hats will feed Judah little white rocks for the pain and teach him how to breathe through the contractions. This will be hard for Judah, because of his asthma.

"Match his breathing," the doctors will say to the girl. "Push and breathe, or your baby will die."

She will try her best, but it will be difficult because, despite her pushing and breathing, allshecanfeelareJudah'sfeetinhisshoesandthewayhisface islikeasheetkickedtothefootofthebed.Afewwarmtearstracetheundulating skinandshewillfeelthesetoo.

The doctor took my hand and led me down the porch, through the rain.

The Honeymooners were curled, wet in a puddle, laughing at their rubber bands. So while they soaked, the doctor plucked a leaf from the ground and twisted it, like wringing the neck of a bird. It became a cone.

"It's a simple surgery," The doctor said.

So I've been told.

"You know," I said to the doctor as she knelt down to touch the Honeymooner's wrists. "They're doing crazy things with science these days." She peeled away a few layers of the skin with a sharpened stone.

"Like what?" she made an unhappy face and carved deeper.

"Flying machines."

She let off a little laugh. "Oh, yes, Marcus and his kites."

In the silence that followed, the doctor slid the small end of the leaf-cone into a bloodied wrist. It worked like a funnel when she tipped the spiders in, although it looked like a child pouring soup in a make believe kitchen.

The jar was actually for jam. The flavor had been strawberry, so the label says.

"I hear your parents aren't fixed?" The doctor didn't look at me when she asked this.

"They're not." I didn't look at her either, only her hands holding steady the invisible drip of spiders.

Whenthetimecomesshewillhaveanaffairwithamaninacoat.

Whileshefeelslimp,Judahwillfeelelectricandcometolovethemanhis wifehasbeenwith.Hewillvisitthedoctorsandbegthemtotakethespidersout.

Please put his *inside me instead.*

Butthedoctorscan'tdothatsohewillleavehiswife,andhateeverynight whenhefeels

hertouchingherselfandocassionallyhervocalcordsmakingthesound, "Judah."

Or maybe,

Oncethey'vegrownoldandgottenusetofeelingthecreasesoftheirown hands,theirchildren(they'vehadthree)willhavetheirownchildrenwhowill askthem.

"Why'd you get fixed?"

Itwassolongagotheywon'thaveananswer.

Inschools,theywillteachthekidsaboutloveandnotaboutsystems.The waysheand Judahlivewillhavebecomeoldfashioned.

"Why'd you get fixed?" Theywillaskagain. "Weren't you afraid you'd miss *feeling* each other?"

"No,no,weweren'tbecausewebelieveinfamilyorganization."

That'sarehearsedanswer.Theydon'tfeelthewordsoneventheirpartner's tongue.

To be fair, it will be hard, at their age, to remember a time when any of this mattered.

Once I confirmed this—my parents weren't fixed—the doctor's muscles stiffened. I could see through her jeans because the fabric was soaked.

"That's an impotent union." The doctor finally turned to face me, and I saw the berry juice on her lips staining them red. The lips went down on both sides like a bridge. "There's no system, no organization, in marriages like that. Families break apart."

So I've been told.

I said, "It seems to work for them."

She said, "Probably not. God didn't want it that way. Unfixed men and women ruin their bodies and their minds and their spirits in sin."

I don't know much about sin. Some people say Marcus is a sinner, and his kites the work of the devil. "My mom and dad are in love." I respond. "I think maybe Judah and I could be like that too."

She stood and put her face very close to mine. Our beads of water and sweat mixed and fell together.

"Well, what does *he* want?"

"To get fixed."

"So get fixed. It's right to do anyhow, and he's the man."

"So? Won't *I* be the man once we're fixed?"

The Honeymooners began to pull at their rubber bands. When the blood flooded back into their fingers, they wailed at the new sensation of transposition and touched each other, all over, in the rain.

The doctor said to me, "Didn't I tell you to be quiet?"

Judah will die first. She will feel nothing but relief.

WE ♥ SHAPES

Jenny Bitner

My son is looking at himself in the mirror. He is five and he likes to see what he looks like, to admire himself a little—the impish grin, the eyes like little suns. I look at the reflection too and am so glad that what I see is a small human boy, with blondish hair and hazel eyes. I'm an octopus, my son says. Look at all my arms, but my son is only pretending to be an octopus, with long soupy tentacles that hang down like tree branches. He moves his arms all around in a dance, and I can almost see his arms becoming tentacles in his mind, but he is playing of course. He isn't really an octopus, today.

My son has problems with shape-shifting. Not that it's a problem. Harwin and Grant proved in 2033 that shape-shifting is not a genetic problem and that it does not have long-term health effects, except maybe to the mothers. Do you know what it's like to have your son turn into a squid when you are nursing him? Or to have your five-year-old suddenly become a monkey? Supposedly as he gets older he will have more ability to control his shift, but for now it's annoying and terrifying.

On his first day of kindergarten he became a scorpion, and the teacher got very angry. She locked him in the closet and stuffed newspaper under the door so he wouldn't get out. When you are a boy again, tell me your name and you can come out, she told him. Unfortunately he became a boy again while they were at recess, and he was so frightened in the closet that he peed his pants. It's OK to lock a scorpion in a closet, but to lock a five-year-old boy in a closet is cruel. I felt terrible for him as he shook with fear that night, telling me about the dark closet and the spiders in there. I can feel for the teacher though. What was she supposed to do, let him sting the other children?

On Tuesdays at three we go to Re-shifting therapy; it's supposed to train Marcus to only shift into positive animals. We sit and watch slides of dogs and cats, and then we try to imagine ourselves becoming dogs and cats. We don't imagine ourselves becoming something that will bite or something that will be easily stepped on and killed. I don't even want to go there. The ant scare. The great ant scare. Never again, I tell him. Never again become an ant. Do you know how afraid I was that someone was going to step on you? We were walking in the street, and he suddenly shifted. A woman's high-heeled shoe came within inches of him before I could grab him. I put him in a jar and let him crawl there until I got home, but what if that happened when I wasn't there?

The re-shifting specialist, Meagan, tells me, Don't put too much emphasis on what he can't be. At his age he can't control it, and he may unconsciously become something to assert power over you.

OK, I say, but you teach him no ants. Please. No scorpions. I can't take it.

Most shape-shifting children make it through childhood without killing anyone or being killed, she says.

Most, I say. But what are some of the bad stories? We are alone, and I want her to tell me the whole truth. I want to know, to brace myself for what is possible.

A rattlesnake who killed his baby sister, but that was an isolated case.

My God. No, no, I say. My God, no. What else? (I act like I haven't read a thousand stories on the Internet about this.)

A girl who became a moth and flew into a candle by mistake, she says, but that's rare, very rare.

I want to cry. I decided not to have any more children after I found out Marcus was a shifter. I too had heard stories like the rattlesnake. In one, a boy became a bear and mauled his brother. The brother lived, but had to have a face transplant. I didn't think it was fair to give Marcus a sibling.

Help him control it, I tell her. It's your job.

You have seen the research, she said, we can start showing him the way, but the ability to control before eight is not possible. It's an involuntary reflex. Try to keep him in safe situations.

But a safe situation for a boy is different than what is safe for an ant or an antelope or a cobra. And safe for us—or safe for him?

At night when we go to sleep, we say a prayer. Now I lay me down to sleep. I pray my self and shape to keep. If I should change before I wake, I pray I will not be a snake.

OK, I made it up for him, but he seems to like it and praying with him eases my mind a little. I say another prayer.

Dear God, Don't let my son become anything unsafe to himself or to anyone else. Let him live to become a man, just a man, not an elephant, or a seal, or a tiger.

Some parents have cages in their houses, those whose children have become tigers or lions. Marcus has never become a large cat. I am debating with my husband whether we should have a cage installed. It costs $5,000 and my husband thinks it's not necessary. He'll be able to control it soon enough, he says, and besides, I think that he's still Marcus inside there and he won't eat us. What about the snake and his sister? I say. That boy was young and he was probably jealous of her. It's unfortunate, but it's just an enactment of childhood jealousy.

What about the Oedipus complex? Ever hear of that? I ask my husband. He might be jealous of you.

Marcus is not going to kill me, my husband says. Don't worry about it.

And so I go along with my life trying not to worry, trying to raise him like a normal boy, and then there is the day of the picnic. We belong to a support group called We ♥ Shapes. It's for children who are shapeshifters, and it's supposed to help them feel more comfortable with their condition. So last month there was a group picnic for the children. Everything was going wonderfully. The children really do seem more comfortable with each other, and more imaginative, sweeter children I have never met, but then after we finished eating (fried chicken, potato salad, fruit salad, and green salad) one of the children out of nowhere turns into a moth. Her mother cried, Oh Sally, and tried to catch her quickly, but then in a flash of an eye, all of the children turned into moths. It's called a spontaneous unconscious mob shift. I had heard about this, but never seen it. Anyway, it was terrifying because now I couldn't tell which one of the moths was Marcus, and there were some other real moths and butterflies flying around too, and we were wildly trying to catch the children, bumping into each other, running after our children (or real moths, since we couldn't tell the difference) and catching them with whatever we could find: red party cups, our hands, a plastic bag with small holes poked in. One of the mothers quickly emptied out a glass jar of pickled eggs and poked holes into the lid. We put all of the moths in there, but I couldn't be sure that we had Marcus. There had been 10 children with us that day, and now we had 12 moths and a butterfly (just to be sure) in the jar, but what if we had missed one of the children and got a real moth by mistake? The child could be stepped on, caught in a tree, fly into a fire. And then there was the fact that the children could never turn back into children in a glass jar. We rushed to one of the parent's houses nearby and let all of the moths free in a room with the windows and doors shut.

One of the mothers didn't want to leave the park. She was sure that we had not caught her son. Ronnie always gets away, she said. He might be here, and then if I leave, I'll never find him. So we left her behind in the park, running after moths, hoping that Ronnie would be OK. We waited in the basement as the children finally, after an hour, started turning back into children. One by one they returned, and one by one I would look for Marcus and it wouldn't be him. One of the children was Ronnie though, and so I held him and comforted him while someone called his mother.

Finally there were only two moths and a butterfly left, and time kept ticking, like when you make microwave popcorn and wait for the last kernels to pop. I sat and waited for the moth to become Marcus, but five then ten minutes passed. My God, I thought: I don't think any of these moths are Marcus; I think I left him behind. And I started to cry. Those aren't children, I said, they are real moths and a real butterfly. Then Ronnie's mother called and said that she had found Marcus high up in a tree and helped him climb down. Thank God, I said. Thank God. Why didn't I have the intuition to know that none of those moths was Marcus? Didn't I even know my own child? I felt like a terrible mother, a mother that left her child alone in a park. It was child abuse, if you could count child abuse against parents of shifters.

They have had to loosen the laws some for the greater good of the community. One particularly difficult case of a girl who turned into a lion almost every day was in the press a lot. Her parents kept her in a cage and fed her there. Psychologists felt that she wasn't getting the social interaction and love that she needed. I can't help it, her mother said, I pet her through the cage, but she almost took off my husband's hand. It's not something we can handle. And so families of shape-shifters have a separate set of laws and are seldom investigated for child abuse. The authorities just want us to keep our children from hurting anyone, however we need to. We reassess how we can be good parents, we scale back.

On Marcus's sixth birthday I am a nervous wreck. The number of things that can go wrong on this day is as high as the mattresses in "The Princess and the Pea" (a story that to me always seems to teach children the wrong message about the need for getting things their way). I try and fail to sleep the night before the event. Marcus is not a night shifter, thank God, and so the hours between 8 PM and 7 AM are usually the golden time when I can relax and not worry, but not in this case. We have never had a birthday party. In years past, everything was too out of control. There were so many medical appointments and trips to the emergency room that we had failed to establish a true circle of friends for him, but now he is a social kindergartener, and he also has his group of friends from We ♥ Shapes. I had invited everyone in kindergarten whose name he could remember.

Needless to say, I wanted to invite all of the children in his support group, but each one was like adding a live grenade to a birthday party. With each one I added to the party list, I was raising the odds that the party would become more like a disaster movie than a celebration. I limited it to his three closest friends: Todd, who rarely shifts, Miles, who always shifts into mild animals like rabbits, and Rosie, a wild card who hasn't shifted that much lately, but has on occasion been a bobcat and a snake (non-poisonous).

All of the children from kindergarten had been trained that Marcus was a shifter. Some have seen him shift, and for the others there was an in-class education program that included reading the classic, *Jimmy*

Becomes a Beaver. It's about a boy that becomes a beaver and how he and his class build a damn together. A feel-good book, but how often does something like that happen? I felt the book downplayed the seriousness of the condition and how dangerous some of the animals are that children become. But the educators said the book was a first step. It helped keep shifters from being stigmatized by other children, and the material used in conjunction with it taught that sometimes shifters could become dangerous animals and advised caution when this occurred. I could see the point, I guess. I didn't want children to fear for their lives around my son, but on the other hand, a healthy dose of fear might save their lives.

The party's theme is trains. Marcus is a bit of a Thomas the Train nut, and I had a cake decorated with Thomas (the eternally useful train), and we took all of his trains and tracks into the backyard to play with. Marcus wanted a bouncy house, so I bit my tongue on the commercial brashness of it and paid men to come into my backyard and blow up a huge plastic monstrosity shaped like a train (the Thomas trademark was not licensed to bouncy houses). Marcus was thrilled. I wish that I could tell you that everything went wonderfully at the party, but Marjorie Lowley's mother would tell her therapist otherwise (they are now being treated for post-traumatic stress disorder). In a certain context, what happened at the party was not so terrible. It depends on your feelings about sex and children.

The cake was just about to be brought out, when out of nowhere Rosie Shapiro became a bonobo. I say that now—bonobo—but at the time all I knew was that she was a monkey, a smallish monkey, that I initially thought I could control. Oh my God, she's shifting, I thought when it happened, because I could see her rapidly becoming stronger and hairier and heavier, and then there was about thirty seconds—when her mother came over to her and tried to take her away—that it seemed like it might be ok, and then the other children shifted. And by other children, I don't mean just Marcus and Miles and Todd, but also another boy from Marcus's kindergarten class who had not even been identified as a shifter, and the doctor would later say had latent shifting tendencies that were exacerbated by the rapid group shifting of four children in his vicinity. And so now there were five monkeys at the party. One of the parents had the Shapeshifter app on his phone, which can identify any animal from a photo, and he quickly took a picture of the monkeys and proclaimed them bonobos. It has a warning, he said. The warnings were flashing notes in red that told parents what the most dangerous thing about the animal was. It says, Warning: Sexually Uninhibited.

The parents went forward towards the children. I grabbed for Marcus's arm to lead him away from the other children, but his arm felt like iron under my hand. He turned to me, put his wrinkly, oversized hand on me and pushed. Jesus, he hit me hard right in the chest. I fell back on my butt. Don't hit me, Marcus, I said, but I could see that he was all bonobo now. The other bonobos broke free from their parents and gathered in the jumpy house.

Unfortunately for Marjorie Lowley, she was still in the jumpy house. The bonobos started to groom each other and then—let me just say for the record that no sexual intercourse occurred—thank God. What did happen was a bit of a touch orgy. The bonobos were grooming each other, and then they approached Marjorie. She must have been influenced by *Jimmy Becomes a Beaver*, because she seemed to not be afraid of them and was very excited at first. They've become monkeys, she said. How cute. Look, the children are all monkeys. Hello monkey, she said, but the bonobos were more interested in her physical presence than her language. They touched her dress, they fondled her hair. They started to rub their genitals against her pretty pink, party dress. Marjorie's mother was just coming back from the bathroom. I can't imagine the shock the scene must have given her. She didn't have a minute to adjust to the fact that the children were bonobos. For all she knew the children had disappeared and been replaced by monkeys. As the scene registered she screamed, No, my baby! and rushed towards the jumpy house.

We all head for the jumpy house. Marjorie's mother grabs Marjorie, her big arm around the pink waist of the girl, and with the strength of a great ape mother, pries her away from the bonobos. Marjorie looks with confusion and horror at the bonobo children, our children, as her mother runs with her screaming to the car.

I make one last attempt to connect with Marcus, to try to pull him out of the animal world and into ours. He is using his mouth to bite bugs off the neck of another bonobo. Marcus, I say, you're my little boy, remember? It's Mommy. I love you. And I take his hand and turn him towards me and try to look deep into his eyes, to see if somewhere inside there my son still exists. He looks at me and his eyes for a second show interest. He reaches out towards me and I think that he might come to me and hug me, but instead he reaches for the top of my dress and puts his hand down the front, under the shirt and bra, and touches my breast, his wrinkly long ape fingers grabbing for my nipple. I push him away instinctively, my hand shoving hard against his hairy chest, and there is a look on his face of surprise and hurt as if he had just been trying to show me his love, and I had rejected him. I am a bad mother, I think, and then he turns away and starts biting bugs off the bonobo's neck again, and I think I should put the ice cream away before it melts. And when I look at him now, even though he is a bonobo, I can still see Marcus in him somewhere, Marcus under and a part of the ape.

All of the parents of human children take them and leave. Most don't even say goodbye; they just walk quickly out the gate. One boy wants a balloon, and tries to go to the other end of the yard to get it, but his mother grabs his hand and runs with him out the gate, telling him she will buy him one later. I know that they will never come to a party at our house again. I know that whatever we try, we will never be a normal family.

I take a deep breath. I realize that instead of horror what I feel is relief—nobody is dead, nobody lost a limb. Marcus hasn't become a tiger and eaten one of the children. I look around at the other mothers and fathers of shifters. They have all attempted, in their way, to bring their children back and failed. We, who have been hurt in so many ways by these children, do not want to be hurt again.

One of the fathers says, There's still cake. One of the mothers spreads out a blanket. We sit on the grass and eat cake as the bonobo children groom and rub each other in the bouncy house.

FLYING CATS (ACTUALLY SWOOPING)

Dan Sklar

A cat in a tree I am a cat in a tree
I feel like a cat in a tree in the future
there will be flying cats,
actually swooping cats as they will
evolve and move up into the trees
and abandoned buildings a world of
swooping cats is a world
I want to see—to see a world where
cats swoop is something
I want to do swooping cats
cats that swoop I want to live
in a world where there are flying
cats and one lands on your shoulder
and meows and does a little cat dance
up there and digs its nails in,
but not enough to hurt and a cat
will sit in a canoe with you
and maybe other cats will swoop in,
meow and fly back into the trees.
Sometimes they catch flying squirrels
but not too often. This is the future
I am thinking of—flying cats in canoes
and bicycles. Sometimes when
you're riding your bike a flying cat
will land on your back, sit down,
look around, knead your back a little,
then fly off. In the future the principal
means of transportation will be horses

and horse-drawn things and bicycles
and walking and trolley cars
and slow trains, not too many motors
for the most part. People will want to
go slowly to places because they want
to see things and think about them
and there is no hurry. In the future
there is no hurry. There are no clocks.
People will figure out time by the sun
and how they feel about it.
There will be a lot of looking at the sky
and stars. It will be a common activity.
There will be many tents. People will
spend more time in tents but mostly
they will be out-of-doors, which will
be better than indoors—even for old people.
Old people will sit outside most of the time
and a cat will land in their lap and they will
pet the cat and the cat will purr and this
will add many out-of-doors sky-looking
years to their lives. There will be many
hammocks in the future, set up for the
old folks when they need to take naps
and when it is time for them to die
and they will know when they will climb
into a hammock and die in the cool
shade on a summer's day.

About the Contributors

aJbishop lives, writes, and runs a business in Montreal, Quebec. She lives with a mastiff named Cooper. "NotSeeing (a contemporary vision)" is excerpted from a larger poem named "The Plane of Consistency" which continues to explore iterating digressions.

Jenny Bitner's work has appeared in *The Sun,* PANK, *Utne Reader,* and *Best American Nonrequired Reading,* among many other publications. She teaches writing at the San Francisco Writers' Grotto.

Steve Castro was born in Costa Rica. He will be attending the MFA Program in Creative Writing at American University in Washington, D.C., starting fall 2013. His work has been nominated for a Pushcart Prize.

Joanne M. Clarkson has authored several collections of poems including *Pacing the Moon* (Chantry Press). She has Master's Degrees in English and Library Science. She has been a teacher and librarian and currently works as a Registered Nurse. Taught by her psychic grandmother, she reads palms and tarot.

Patrick Cole lives in Barcelona. His fiction appeared recently in *Conclave* and *Timber* and has also been published in *Parcel, High Plains Literary Review, Nimrod International, Agni online, Knock, 34th Parallel,* and *turnrow.* He has received two Pushcart nominations.

Thia Li Colvin lives far to the west of the western U.S., with her two daughters and husband. By day, she writes magazine features. Her nights are her own.

David Ellis Dickerson is a regular contributor to "This American Life." A former greeting card writer, he often appears on public radio offering commentary about cards and holidays. But what he really wants to do is write strange stories.

LaTasha N. Nevada Diggs is a writer and musician and the author of *TWERK* (Belladonna, 2013). Her poetry has appeared in *Ploughshares, Jubilat, Fence, Rattapallax, Nocturnes,* and *LA Review.* She has received scholarships, residencies, and fellowships from Cave Canem, Harvestworks Digital Media Arts Center, and New York Foundation for the Arts, among others. She is a native of Harlem.

Molly English is a writer and illustrator from the northwest suburbs of Chicago. She is currently pursuing a BFA in studio art and creative writing at the University of Iowa.

Mariev Finnegan lives in a Gothic house on the dead end of Erie Street, on the edge of the Erie Canal, with her grandson, Jacob Stump; a three-legged dog, Bloody Stump; Erie, the cat; and an owl named Who?

Erin Fitzgerald's writing has appeared, or is forthcoming, in publications such as *The Rumpus, Hobart, Salt Hill, PANK, Wigleaf, Artifice,* and *FRiGG.* Her chapbook *This Morning Will Be Different* appeared in the anthology *Shut Up/Look Pretty* (Tiny Hardcore Press, 2012). Erin lives in western Connecticut.

Soren Gauger is a Canadian who has lived for over a decade in Krakow. He has published two books, *Hymns to Millionaires* (Twisted Spoon Press) and *Quatre Regards sur l'Enfant Jesus* (Ravenna Press), and many translations of Polish writers. He wrote the story included here first in Polish and then translated it.

Libby Hart is an Australian poet with two books of poetry: *Fresh News from the Arctic* and *This Floating World.* She is a Pushcart nominee and the recipient of several fellowships, including the DJ O'Hearn Memorial Fellowship, and residencies in Australia and Europe.

Liana Holmberg writes prose and poetry. Her work has appeared in the Academy of American Poets anthology *New Voices* and journals including *Mānoa, Hawai'i Review,* and *decomP magazinE.* Liana is the founding editor and publisher at Red Bridge Press. She grew up along a rural coast in Hawai'i and now lives in San Francisco.

Catie Jarvis received her MFA in fiction and poetry from California College of the Arts. She grew up on a lake in New Jersey and now lives by the ocean in Marina del Rey, California. She finds the world to be a strange place.

With a PhD in literature from the University of Texas at Austin, Dr. **Michelle S. Lee** headed for the Atlantic coast where she now teaches composition and creative writing at Daytona State College. Her work has appeared in publications ranging from *Text and Performance Quarterly* to *Northwind Magazine.*

Norman Lock has written fiction, as well as stage and radio plays. He won *The Paris Review* Aga Kahn Prize and fellowships from the New Jersey Council on the Arts and the National Endowment for the Arts. *Love Among the Particles* (Bellevue Literary Press) is his newest story collection.

Jønathan Lyons lives and writes in Central Pennsylvania. He teaches writing and literature at Bucknell University. His work has appeared in the *Journal of Experimental Fiction, Hotel Amerika, Exquisite Corpse,* and elsewhere. He received an MFA from California College of the Arts.

Robert Neilson's first short story sale was in 1989. Since then he has sold over a hundred more, a graphic novel, two short story collections, some comics, three radio plays, a book on crystals, reviews, interviews and has found time to edit *Albedo One* magazine. He is married with children and lives in Ireland.

Born in Scotland, **John Newman** moved to Canada as a teenager and has lived in Ottawa, Ontario, for 25 years. A graduate of Carleton University with a BA in English Literature, John is predominantly a screenwriter and has sold and optioned a number of short scripts and feature length screenplays.

Christina Olson is the author of a book of poems, *Before I Came Home Naked.* Recent writing has appeared, or is forthcoming, in *The Southern Review, River Styx, Gastronomica,* RHINO, and *Hobart.* She is the poetry editor of *Midwestern Gothic,* and lives in Georgia.

Zach Powers lives and writes in Savannah, Georgia. His stories have appeared all over the place, and his writing for television won an Emmy. He is the founder and co-host of the literary arts nonprofit Seersucker Live.

Jordan Reynolds has published poems, essays and reviews in *Interim, The Offending Adam, zero ducats, The Agriculture Reader,* and elsewhere. He lives in San Francisco.

Sharif Shakhshir was born and raised in Pomona, California. He is the Editor in Chief at the *Southern California Review* and a graduate student at the University of Southern California, where he studies fiction, poetry, and screenwriting

At Endicott College, **Dan Sklar** teaches his students to love language and to write in an original, natural, and spontaneous way. Recent publications include *Harvard Review, New York Quarterly, Ibbetson Street Press,* and *The Art of the One Act.*

Deborah Steinberg's writing has been published in *Shelflife, Café Irreal, Blood and Thunder,* and other journals. A founding editor of Red Bridge Press, she lives in San Francisco, where she facilitates writing workshops with a focus on healing. She also sings in the women's a cappella group Conspiracy of Venus.

Wendy Patrice Williams blogs inspiring words of healing that help people cope with early trauma and post-traumatic stress. An excerpt from her memoir manuscript, *The Autobiography of a Sea Creature*, appears in *The Healing Art of Writing* (University of California Press).

xTx is a writer living in Southern California. She has been published in places like *The Collagist, PANK, Hobart, Puerto del Sol, Smokelong, Monkeybicycle,* and *Wigleaf.* Her story collection "Normally Special" (Tiny Hardcore Press) and her chapbook *Billie the Bull* (Mud Luscious Press) are now available.

Rachel Yoder edits *draft: the journal of process* which features first and final drafts of stories, essays, and poetry along with author interviews. She holds MFAs in Fiction and Creative Nonfiction. She was an Iowa Arts Fellow and received the 2012 *Missouri Review* Editors' Prize in Fiction. The essay included here is from her manuscript *The Hard Problem: A Guide for the Intergalactic Writer Looking To Mate.*

Edmund Zagorin is a writer and argument coach in Iowa City, Iowa, and Detroit, Michigan. His serial novel *Sorry, Our Unicorn Has Rabies* appears regularly on Jukepop. For those who enjoy physical correspondence, Edmund mails the free monthly broadsheet *Stories By Mail.*

Olga Zilberbourg was born in St. Petersburg, Russia, and moved to the United States at the age of seventeen. Her English-language writing has appeared in *Narrative Magazine, Santa Monica Review, eleven eleven Journal, Mad Hatters Review, J Journal, Prick of the Spindle,* and HTMLGiant. Olga is a senior associate editor at *Narrative Magazine.*

For more information on these authors, visit redbridgepress.com/authors.

Acknowledgments

We thank the Red Bridge Press team for the rich insights and countless hours they put into this book: Lavonne Leong, Seth Amos, Charles Kermit Playfoot, Josh McDonald, and Barry Dixon. We are grateful to our families for their patience and support. And to Alex Dailey and Ian Liffmann: Thanks for having our backs.

The quote from Rumi's poem "Moses and the Shepherd" that appears in "NotSeeing (a contemporary vision)" by aJbishop is used with permission of the translator Coleman Barks.

Dear Reader,

Thank you for reading this book! We loved making it for you.

Red Bridge Press is an independent publisher of print books and ebooks. Our mission is to bring you the best in genre-bending, border-crossing literature that electrifies and inspires you.

We hope you enjoyed *Writing That Risks* and will recommend it to friends. In fact, we hope you'll recommend it to strangers. Lots of them. Please take a moment to post a review at book retail sites online (e.g. Amazon, Barnes & Noble) and recommendation sites like Goodreads. If you're a blogger or journalist and want to write a story about the book, contact us at editors@ redbridgepress.com.

Your voice matters. Thank you for helping us spread the word about these authors and their delightful, daring work.

Yours truly,
Liana Holmberg
& the Red Bridge Press team

CPSIA information can be obtained at www.ICGtesting.com
Printed in the USA
BVOW10s1837180715

408909BV00019B/153/P